HER ONE-NIGHT PRINCE

Rebecca J. Clark

ROMANCE

BookStrand
www.BookStrand.com

A SIREN-BOOKSTRAND TITLE
IMPRINT: Romance

HER ONE-NIGHT PRINCE
Copyright © 2011 by Rebecca J. Clark

ISBN-10: 1-61926-299-1
ISBN-13: 978-1-61926-299-7

First Printing: December 2011

Cover design by Jinger Heaston
All cover art and logo copyright © 2011 by Siren Publishing, Inc.

Printed in the U.S.A.

PUBLISHER
www.BookStrand.com

DEDICATION

To Dan—if we'd gone to the same high school, you'd have dated my sister. She was the beautiful cheerleader, and you were captain of the football team *and* the baseball team. I was just…a nobody. But I would've had a major crush on you and written about you in my diary. I'm glad I met you *after* high school.

To all my readers who weren't in the popular crowd in high school—aren't you glad those days are long gone?

HER ONE-NIGHT PRINCE

REBECCA J. CLARK

Chapter 1

All Mitch knew about her was her first name, Lydia.

He wondered for the umpteenth time how he'd let himself be talked into this nonsense. She might as well have used the age-old description for a less-than-attractive blind date by telling him she had a good personality.

But this was no blind date, just a bad idea.

He sipped an iced latte as he scanned the eclectic crowd gathered for Alive After Five, a weekly event in downtown Boise highlighted by live music and a sampling of foods from local eateries. All around him scads of people sat, mingled, danced, and ate amidst a sea of brightly colored umbrellas. How could he find anyone in this melee, let alone someone for whom he had no description?

Leaning against a large planter, he tried to imagine what a woman would look like who needed to advertise for a date to her class reunion. The feeling in his gut sank like the Titanic.

His attention skirted the skyline to the sun-burnished foothills beyond. Beautiful evenings like this practically begged him to take his Harley for a leisurely ride along a winding mountain road, into the open spaces of Mother Nature. A frown tugged at the corners of his mouth. But no. He was stuck here waiting for Lydia, wherever the hell she was.

He checked his watch. In five more minutes the fun would begin.

If he didn't owe a friend this favor, he could be halfway up the mountain by now. His buddy, Hal, a reporter at a local newspaper, was writing a series of articles about dating in the age of the Internet and social networking. Currently researching ads on Craigslist, he'd cashed in favors from several friends by asking them to respond to ads for his story.

Today was Mitch's turn. Hooray.

In the center of the square, jets of water sprung up from the ground in random spurts. The playful fountain was hard to resist in this hottest month of the year. Mitch watched in distracted amusement the young kids and not-so-young kids dodging and running through the water, their squeals and shrieks of laughter barely discernible over the sounds of the sixties-rock band jamming on the makeshift stage across the square.

A line of perspiration trickled down his temple, and he wished he'd worn shorts rather than Levi's and a T-shirt. He gulped the latte, and the ice slid down his throat, bringing only slight relief. He'd give Lydia a few more minutes. Then he was out of here.

While enviously watching the fountain antics, he noticed a woman staring at him through the spray. He met her gaze. That couldn't possibly be Lydia, could it? Her rigid and unfriendly posture matched her formidable attire, a coldly professional pantsuit that had to be unbearable in this heat. Blonde hair swept back off her face in a tight bun, and she glared at him over wire-rimmed glasses.

Hiking the strap of a substantial black purse over her shoulder, she started toward him, deflating his bubble of hope that she wasn't Lydia. Damn. She wasn't at all what he'd expected. He'd *expected* a shy, mousy type. He'd *fantasized* a voluptuous, knockout type—hey, a guy could dream, couldn't he? But this woman was neither.

She circled the fountain and stopped in front of him, flicking an icy blue gaze over him just as coolly as he'd assessed her. Mitch felt a twinge of uneasiness, unused to being on the receiving end of such a critical look. Worse, she looked him almost straight in the eye. With him at six foot three, he figured she must be five feet ten or so without shoes.

He gave her his most charming grin, one that had never before failed him with women, and all it got him was, "*You're* Mitch Gannon?" as if he was nothing more than a piece of gum on the sole of her sensible shoes.

The sexy timbre of her voice sure didn't match the woman, and it caught him off guard. He didn't remember that from their brief phone call. "Uh, yeah."

She wrinkled up her nose and studied him head to toe. "You're the man who answered my ad." It wasn't a question.

Could her disappointment be any more obvious? Who'd she been expecting? Bradley Cooper? If this was any indication of her bedside manner, no wonder the woman couldn't get a date by conventional means.

"You're not at all what I expected," she said.

The feeling's mutual. Had he forgotten to use deodorant this morning? From her distasteful expression, he might have skipped that step of his routine.

Man, Hal was going to owe *him* after this.

"I'm Lydia St. Clair," she said before he thought of a civil response to her statement. She motioned to her right. "There's shade next to the buildings." Pivoting that direction, she obviously expected him to follow.

With a bemused grin, he did. Her long legs carried her quickly across the pavement, her practical heels clicking against the red brick.

As to the rest of her figure, it was hard to tell under that shapeless pantsuit, which was the ugliest, flattest shade of gray he'd ever seen. It was battleship gray and buttoned to the collar, fending off all possibilities of attack.

He cocked an eyebrow. No threat here.

This person definitely didn't match that voice.

Lydia led him to a slightly quieter spot in the shade of the Bank of America Center. She unzipped her bag and rifled through it. As she did, Mitch found himself peering down at her pale-blonde hair, looking for dark roots. The color was too incredible to be real.

He studied her as she concentrated on the contents of her purse, the writer in him trying to get a feel for this woman. The man in him thought of a definite way to know if she was a natural blonde. He checked his thoughts. She wasn't his type—not even close—but here he was picturing her naked.

Lydia raised her head, and he returned her cool stare with a shamefaced smile as if she'd read his thoughts. She didn't return the smile.

BlackBerry in hand, she pressed a series of buttons. "I have a couple of questions for you."

"Shoot." Then he'd have a couple of questions for Hal's stupid story, and he was out of here. The only thing even remotely likable about her was her voice. It belonged on someone wild, someone sexy, someone who didn't pull her hair back like that. It belonged to a lady who wasn't afraid to be a woman.

Something on her jacket caught his eye. A piece of white material stuck out between two buttons over her chest. Wayward lingerie, perhaps? He squinted. No. It was too stiff and unyielding. He imagined Lydia St. Clair starching her panties, and smirked.

When he lifted his gaze, he found her staring at him. Glaring was more like it. Realizing she assumed he'd been checking her out, Mitch sipped from his drink, hoping the moment would pass gracefully.

It wasn't his lucky day.

"You *are* gay, aren't you?" she asked.

His mouthful of latte spewed like a torpedo yet somehow missed drenching her. Was she serious? One look at her stony face told him she was.

He'd been accused of many things in his life. Being gay wasn't one of them. The idea was so far-fetched he couldn't help grinning. He wiped his chin with the back of his wrist. "Gee, is it that obvious?"

"Actually, I'd never have guessed except for the ad."

He frowned. "The ad?"

"You know, that it was in the Men Seeking Men section?"

His teeth clenched. *Hal.* He was a dead man. The joker probably sat in his office right now, laughing his ass off.

Suddenly, the hilarity of the situation hit Mitch, and he concentrated to keep a straight face. "Oh," he said. "Right."

Lydia watched him, her expression wary. "So…you *are*, right?" No judgment tinged her voice, just curiosity and something sounding an awful lot like hope.

He stifled a grin. He cocked a brow and stared her square in the eye. Why not have some fun with this? After a few more minutes, he'd never see her again. Obviously, Hal didn't want a story here, just payback for setting him up on a recent and disastrous blind date. Mitch should have expected as much when Hal approached him about the lame article he was researching.

"Let me put it this way, Lydia. My last lover's name was Eddie, and my longtime companion, Jacque, is waiting for me at home."

He wasn't lying, exactly. He didn't actually *say* he was gay. Edwina was his last lover, and Jacque was his pet parrot.

Lydia stared at him for a long moment, then her demeanor relaxed tenfold, and she smiled at him. The dour and prim woman was an attractive young lady.

She touched his arm, her long fingers wrapping softly around his wrist. "I can't tell you how relieved I am to hear you say that. You had me worried."

"Huh?" He was so blinded by the change in her that her words barely registered.

She cleared her throat. "When I first saw you, you just didn't look like you're—not that there's a certain way to look—but you didn't act like you're—" A blush swept up her neck and onto her face. "Have I completely put my foot in my mouth yet? I mean, if you'd seen some of the other men who responded to my ad...well, let's just say they weren't as, um, masculine as you." She dropped her gaze, still blushing profusely.

His head firmly reattached to his neck, Mitch smirked and puffed out his chest. Dropping his voice a notch, he said, "Yes, I pride myself on looking like a manly man."

She laughed, and the sound shot straight to his groin. God. It was even sexier than her voice.

"The way you look made me think I'd approached the wrong man, and then when I caught you looking at my—" She cleared her throat again.

He nodded his understanding even though he had absolutely no clue what—Oh. "I wasn't staring at your, ah, chest." He cocked his head and motioned to her jacket. "You have something caught in the buttons."

Narrowing those pale blue eyes, she glanced down, then immediately back up, pressing her hand to her chest.

"What's wrong?"

She shook her head and closed her eyes.

"Lydia?"

After a moment, she held out something stiff and white for him to see—a fabric softener sheet. So much for the starched undies image.

Lydia's shoulders drooped. "I am such a social moron," she said. "I can't even dress myself properly."

It occurred to him that she wasn't unfriendly, just very shy. "It's no big deal. It could have been worse."

Her expression conveyed doubt.

"It could have been your panties."

Her eyes widened, and for a moment she said nothing. Then she giggled. God. Viagra had nothing on her laugh. "You're right. I guess it could have been worse."

They shared a few moments of somewhat-awkward silence. "Back to the reason we're here," she began. "Are you free the third Saturday in August?"

"The third Saturday...?" Mitch murmured, his mind not computing.

She nodded. "The night of my reunion."

"Oh. Yeah." Duh.

"The addendum to that question is, are you willing to go with me? Like I told you on the phone, I'd pay for your time."

Mitch thought quickly for a white lie that wouldn't hurt her feelings. Then he remembered he'd be out of town. For some reason, he felt like he was lying when he told her he'd be gone that weekend.

Lydia's expression melted, taking her smile with it.

"I'm sorry." For some reason, he really was. Uncharacteristically feeling the need to explain himself, he said, "Every year in August, some college buddies and I do a cross-country road trip on our bikes, er, motorcycles. This year we leave the weekend of your reunion."

"You might have mentioned that when we spoke on the phone. It would have spared us both this waste of time." Snippiness had returned to her voice.

Yes, he should have, Mitch silently agreed, had he been serious about answering her ad. Sudden anger surged inside him toward Hal for getting him into this mess and putting him in the position of hurting this woman's feelings.

"I'm sorry," he said again. Since when was he into apologizing so much? "It didn't occur to me."

He took the final drink from the latte, melting ice and all, then crumpled the plastic cup in his fist and tossed it into a nearby trash can.

A slight breeze blew in mist from the fountain. A minute droplet settled on one of Lydia's long black lashes. When she blinked, it disappeared.

"Well. I guess I knew it was too good to be true," she said just loudly enough for him to hear over the music. She brushed away a wisp of hair that had fallen onto her forehead. Thrusting out her hand, she said, "It was nice meeting you, Mitch. Thanks for braving the heat wave to come down here."

He shook her hand and felt like a world-class ass. She looked so disappointed. Instead of dropping her hand, he gave it a tug. "Come on," he said on impulse.

She eyed their joined hands. "Where?"

"I'm going to buy you a drink."

"I don't drink."

"An iced tea then."

She jerked her hand free and rubbed it against her slacks, as if to rub off his touch. "Why?"

"Because I was a jerk and wasted your time. I'd like to make it up to you."

* * * *

She had no life.

She'd been resisting that notion for some time now, but today's fiasco pretty much said it all.

Lydia nudged her wire-rimmed glasses into place as she walked beside Mitch. Nerves danced around her belly like skittish mice. What the heck was she doing? She should have just gone home.

Her expectations hadn't been overly high today, due to the other responses she'd gotten to her ad. She hadn't expected Mitch to be a prince, but charming would be nice. He *was* charming. He just wasn't available to be *her* prince.

"Aren't you hot in that suit?" he asked, the din from Alive After Five lessening with every step.

"Yes." Actually, she was sweltering. Her slacks hung hot against her legs, and her feet slid in her pumps. A normal person wouldn't have dressed like this today. A normal person wouldn't have taken out the ad.

"Where do you work, Lydia?"

"I'm a paralegal for Finch and Stanley."

"What exactly does a paralegal do?"

"In my case it means I spend my days in the law library with my nose stuck in a law book."

"Sounds exciting."

She shrugged off his sarcasm. "It pays the bills." It paid most of them anyway.

Mitch said nothing more, and they walked along the sidewalk in silence until they arrived at Amelia's Bar and Grill. Air-conditioning blasted them as they entered the restaurant, and Lydia almost sighed her relief.

She bit back her disappointment when the hostess seated them on the patio. Fortunately, large umbrellas shaded them from the sun and kept the air cool. Mitch pulled out Lydia's chair for her as she sat down. A prompt waitress appeared for their orders and flirted with Mitch. She couldn't blame the girl. He surely had that effect on most women. She pressed her lips together. And men.

Mitch ordered a Budweiser for himself and a tall iced tea for her. He certainly didn't look gay. Oh, she knew there wasn't a certain way to look—just as she'd told him—but the other men who'd answered her ad...well, they fit the stereotype all too well. When she first saw Mitch standing beyond the fountains looking more gorgeous and masculine than should be legal, she didn't even consider that *he* might be the man she was supposed to meet. It was only his T-shirt and his drink—he'd told her on the phone he'd be wearing a Boise State shirt and drinking an iced latte—and the fact that he'd been staring at her, that clued her in. It wasn't often that men stared at her. She couldn't remember the last time, in fact.

Water gurgled in a nearby rock fountain, and large-leaf plants made for a casual yet elegant ambiance. Lydia couldn't help noticing admiring looks coming Mitch's way from various female patrons, and more than a couple of critical once-overs directed at her, as if the women were astounded a man like him would be with a frumpy woman like her. If they only knew the real reason they were together.

"What's so funny?" Mitch asked, startling her. She hadn't realized she was grinning.

"I'm just noticing all the female attention you're getting. I suppose you're used to it. You're very handsome." She recalled her mother's standard joke about the good ones being married or gay. It was probably one of the last pieces of wisdom her mom had dispensed upon her before she died ten years ago.

God had played a cruel trick upon the female population when he'd created Mitch Gannon. From his twinkling dark eyes that seemed to find humor in everything, to the sexy shadow of growth on his strong chin, to his long, muscular legs with jeans fitting just snug enough to enhance, but loose enough not to boast—Mitch was everything a woman could want in a man.

Mitch's brows lifted, and he glanced around their surroundings and puffed out his chest again. "All those manly man lessons must be working."

She laughed. This was kind of fun. These women were envious of *her*. They just assumed she and Mitch were a couple. It was such an odd feeling. When was the last time she'd been on a date with such a handsome man? When had she last been on a date with *any* man? Okay, so this wasn't exactly a date. She knew for certain it had been more than five years, before she'd moved home to take care of her dad.

Leaning forward, Mitch said in a low voice, "This is probably none of my business, Lydia, but as I've never been one to mind my own business, being that I'm a bartender and a writer, I'm going to ask anyway. Why do you want a gay man for a date to your reunion?"

Lydia dipped her head, and a blush warmed her cheeks. Of course he'd ask that. The real question, however, that he was obviously too polite to ask was, *What's wrong with you, and why are you so desperate that you'd resort to the gay personal ads?*

"It's been a long time since I was in the dating scene," she said. Okay, it had been more like *forever*. "I don't want to deal with the romantic complications of asking a straight man."

He stared at her as if he knew that wasn't the whole story. "And you don't want to go alone?"

She shook her head. "If I do, it would just prove to everyone they were right about me."

His brows furrowed. "What do you mean?"

The waitress brought their drinks. When she left, Lydia realized Mitch was waiting for her answer. "I was voted 'Least Likely To' my senior year."

"Least likely to…what?" he asked. She saw when he figured it out. "Oh. You mean—?"

She nodded. "If I show up alone…" She shrugged. "I'd rather not go at all in that case."

"So you're looking for a manly man to accompany you?"

She couldn't help smiling at him, which was an odd thing. She'd probably smiled more with him in the past half hour than she had in the entire past year. Usually, she was such a sourpuss.

"You don't have any male friends you could ask?"

She shook her head.

"No handsome hotshot attorney in your firm?"

Picturing the few single lawyers in her office, Lydia crinkled her nose. "None that I'd want to spend time alone with."

Mitch took a long swig of his beer, eyeing her the entire time over the rim. She would love to know his thoughts. On second thought, she wouldn't. It would most certainly not be flattering. The terms "pathetic" and "hard up" were probably involved.

She reached for her iced tea. Condensation dripped from the tall, narrow glass onto her fingers, then the tabletop. Silence reached between her and Mitch. She wasn't one for small talk and had never been a person who inspired great conversation in anyone.

What was she doing here? She was sitting in a restaurant with a strange man she'd met via the personals—the *gay* personals—talking about her life, or lack thereof. The only thing she'd accomplished today was to embarrass herself.

She set down the tea, pushed her chair back, and stood. "I have to get home." She glanced at her watch and panicked. She *really* had to get home.

"Lydia." Mitch stood and circled the table. "I wish I could help you out."

"Do you have a magic wand to conjure up a one-night Prince Charming for me?"

He shook his head. "But I own a pub off Main Street called The Alley. I don't think any of my customers are royalty, but some of them are nice guys." He smirked.

He clearly thought she was a charity case. Her stomach knotted, and she forced a smile. "Thanks for the offer, but I'll figure something out."

Chapter 2

Lydia held open the screen with her hip as she inserted the key into the lock of the back door. She blew upward onto her forehead, trying to move the strand of hair that kept falling onto her face. It didn't budge, stuck to her skin with perspiration from this god-awful heat and this god-awful suit.

Her dad's caregiver sat at the kitchen table, purse in hand and a scowl on her face as she stared pointedly at the clock on the stove.

Lydia winced. "Sorry I'm late, Alberta. I'll pay you ex—"

The plump, middle-aged woman stood, shaking her head. "I don' want no extra money, Miss Lydia." She pointed toward the front of the house. "*He* is a terrorist. I canna watch him for you no more." She shook her head again, her tidy salt-and-pepper bun not stirring with the movement.

Lydia cut across the room, her heels tapping dully on the checkerboard floor tiles. "Oh, Alberta. Please don't quit on me. I need you." Alberta was the latest in a string of sitters they'd had recently.

Alberta ignored the plea and moved past her, patting Lydia's arm as she went. "God bless you, honey. You seem like a nice girl. I don' know what you did to deserve that monster."

The screen door slammed behind her as she left. Lydia stared at the door for a long moment then turned. The chair Alberta had vacated was at an angle to the oak table, beckoning her. Even though she really didn't have time to sit, she sat anyway and slipped off her shoes, the cool floor tiles luxurious against her tired feet. She tugged off her glasses and rubbed the bridge of her nose.

Feeling slightly better, she reached for the stack of today's mail in the middle of the table. She sighed as she riffled through the medical bills and insurance statements for her father. At the bottom of the pile was an envelope from her alma mater with the word "REMINDER" stamped across the front. *Visit our page on Facebook,* it read.

Her blasted class reunion. She crumpled the notice and dropped it, unopened, into the wastepaper basket beneath the desk. Her gaze found the original invitation thumbtacked to the corkboard above the computer. Taking it down, she stared at it through narrowed eyes, her memory bank shuffling through images of former classmates like a deck of playing cards—Cissy McAllister, Roger Gilmore, Stacy Tillman. She grimaced as their faces, and others, filled the frame in her mind, remembering their cruel pranks and unkind words just because they were popular and she wasn't, just because she'd been gawky and extremely shy. If she attended her reunion, she would very likely see her tormentors again. Did she really want to put herself through that?

It was pointless to worry about. She didn't want to go alone, but she had no one to go with, end of story. She'd told herself before her meeting with Mitch Gannon that if he didn't pan out, she'd give up on the personal ad thing. She didn't need to be bonked in the head with the futility of trying again. It had been a stupid idea anyway.

Sighing, she tacked the invitation back onto the corkboard. As for visiting the Facebook page? Uh, no. She didn't need another reminder of how lacking she was in friends these days. Social media implied being social. She didn't have time for social.

"Hey!" came a shout from the living room. "Hey, hey, hey!" More mumbled words followed then a shuffling sound and a crash. Lydia sighed. What favorite vase or knickknack had he broken now?

Starting across the room, she recalled what Alberta had said about her father, calling him a terrorist and a monster. She supposed she should be offended by that, and at one time she would have been, but it was hard to argue with the truth.

A few hours later, her dad tucked into bed and sleeping peacefully for the moment, Lydia flopped facedown on her bed. After several minutes, unmoving, she pushed herself into a seated position and scooted back against the pillows and headboard.

Looking around the simply furnished room, she sighed. Everything was pretty much the same as it had been growing up— same ratty teddy bear, same bookshelf, same family photos from way back when. Everything was familiar. Not much had changed, including her.

Sure, she was older, and probably wiser, and maybe her hair had grown out from a horrid pixie cut, but other than that, how was she different from the girl who'd grown up in this room?

She picked up Mr. Rex, her old teddy bear, and ran her finger over his good eye. The girl she'd been had dreams for her future. She'd wanted to make something of herself, get away from her gawky teenaged self, move beyond her nerdy image. As her dorkiness with Mitch Gannon proved, however, she still had a lot of room for growth in that area.

Mitch's image floated into her mind, and she smiled. He'd been so nice to her. She wondered briefly what would have happened if that really had been a date at Amelia's. If he was straight and actually interested in *her*, would he have held her hand? Would he have wrapped her in his strong arms and kissed her when the date was over?

Her lips tingled at the thought, and her face heated up in embarrassment. She was fantasizing about a gay man, for heaven's sake. Was she pathetic or what?

For better or worse, she was stuck in the life she had, living in a sort of time warp from which there was no immediate escape. She wasn't complaining. Much. She loved her dad and would do anything for him, yet…She thought again of her class reunion and the invitation hanging downstairs. She'd wanted so badly to go there and pretend for *just one night* she was someone else, kind of like Cinderella.

Cinderella had a fairy godmother. Lydia had no such thing. She held up Mr. Rex, stared at him a moment, then tossed him onto the pillows. No one was going to wave a magic wand and transform her into a beautiful princess. Fairies didn't exist.

She straightened suddenly, her mouth curving into a slight smile. Or did they?

* * * *

Hal King strode between the tables at The Alley, a dumb grin on his face. Obviously, he'd come in to gloat. He sat down at the bar.

"You think you're pretty funny, don't you?" Mitch said, wiping the counter and swiping the wet rag against his former friend's hands.

Hal jerked his hands away and chuckled. "I don't think. I know."

Mitch tossed the rag beneath the counter and poured Hal his usual, waiting as he took a long swig. "Taste okay? No metallic aftertaste?" He filled a frosty mug with Budweiser for another customer.

Hal peered into his half-empty glass as if he hadn't thought about that particular type of retribution. Then he grinned. "You gotta admit, I got you good."

"Overkill, don't you think, King?"

"No way, man. It was perfect payback for setting me up with Wanda or Wendy or whatever her name was."

Mitch shrugged. "I thought she'd be perfect for you. You're a creative guy, a newspaper man. She was a makeup artist." He smirked. "A perfect match."

"She did makeup for *dead people*. I hardly call that a creative profession."

Mitch chuckled. "But now we're even."

"I guess. For now. So tell me about the ad chick?" He finished his beer and pushed the empty glass toward Mitch, signaling he was ready for another.

Accustomed to his friend's chauvinistic attitude, Mitch usually ignored it. Tonight, for some reason, it grated on him like fingernails on a chalkboard. "She wasn't a 'chick.'" He handed Hal the new beer.

Hal sipped it and eyed him over the rim, wiping the foam mustache from his top lip with the back of his wrist. "Do I detect a note of defensiveness there, Gannon?"

Mitch mixed up a dry martini for an order from one of the cocktail waitresses.

"Good-looking?"

Mitch hesitated. "In her own way."

Hal clicked his tongue twice. "Okay. Gotcha. New subject."

Hal started on about the Mariners' chance of making it to the play-offs this year—many Idahoans were big Seattle baseball fans, as the state had no major league teams of its own—but Mitch barely listened. His mind was stuck on Lydia, and he couldn't figure out why. Besides not being attracted to her—although she *was* attractive in her own way, as he'd told Hal, *and* she had the sexiest voice he'd ever heard—she wasn't even close to the type of woman he typically dated. Call him shallow or one-track-minded, but he preferred the drop-dead gorgeous type, with a body to die for, who just liked to have a good time for one night, one week, or however long it took them to tire of each other. He wasn't interested in brainy, conservative types like Lydia. Women like her only served to complicate his simple life. So why couldn't he stop thinking about her? Maybe it was her desperation and her loneliness. Maybe she reminded him of how he used to feel, before he'd simplified his life…

He placed a Chablis, a gin and tonic, and a lemon-drop martini on a tray and signaled to Edwina.

"Hey there, gorgeous," she said, sidling up to the bar in black leather shorts and white blouse. Edwina Shea was a knockout from head to toe, total sex incarnate. "Could you hand me my Coke? I'm dying for a drink."

He reached under the bar and grabbed the cola he kept filled for her throughout her shift. The woman was a caffeine junkie.

She took a long swig, her flame-tipped fingernails wrapped around the tall glass. Bright-red lipstick left a smudge on the rim. She held it out to him. "Want some?"

Mitch shook his head and took the glass from her, putting it back under the bar.

She laughed. "God, you're such a wuss about that."

Hal's ears perked up at the insult. "What? Hmm? Gannon's a wuss?"

Edwina grabbed the tray of drinks and balanced them on her open palm. "He won't drink out of the same glass or share food with me, like he's afraid of cooties." She laughed. "He had no problem sleeping with me, but he'd never share food with me. Go figure. That drove me *crazy* when we dated." She turned away.

Hal's gaze followed the sway of her hips. "Sex and food. Two completely different needs."

"Go screw yourself, King," she shot back sort of good-naturedly.

"Would if I could," Hal replied, turning back to Mitch. "She have some sort of incurable disease or something?"

Mitch shot him a look. "I hate sharing food with anyone. So sue me. Maybe it comes from having had to share everything with all my kid brothers and sisters growing up, but I just can't do it. If I ever meet a woman I could share an ice-cream cone with, I'll marry her."

"Yeah, when pigs fly," Edwina quipped, overhearing the remark as she returned with a tray of dirty glasses. Glancing at Hal, she said, "You know he won't date a woman with children, don't you?"

Hal shrugged. "Yeah. So?"

"So, unless he's into college coeds, that leaves out ninety percent of the single female population, which means the chances of Romeo here ever tyin' the knot are about one in a million."

Mitch rolled his eyes. "I never said I won't date a woman with a child."

"Uh-huh," Edwina remarked. "Name the last single mother you

dated."

"You."

"Yeah, and you broke up with me." She grabbed her tray of drinks and headed out onto the floor.

Hal swiveled his head to check out her ass. "Man oh man, I still think you were nuts to break up with her, kid or not."

Mitch watched Edwina flirt with a table of suits. "It was mutual."

"Not what I heard."

Mitch shot his friend a quizzical look, but Hal didn't elaborate except to say, "Whatever your reason, I still think you're nuts. *I'd* do her in a heartbeat."

"You'd do a blow-up doll in a heartbeat."

Hal raised his eyebrows, smiled a cat-that-ate-the-canary smile, and hopped off his stool. Slapping a few bills onto the bar, he said, "Later, Gannon."

The Friday-afternoon crowd wouldn't thicken for at least another hour, so Mitch set about inventorying the bar. Not the most exciting task in the world, but it beat sitting in a cubicle and staring at a computer screen for twelve hours a day like he'd done at Micron for the ten longest years of his life.

Edwina spoke from behind him. "I need a Bud on tap and a tonic water."

Mitch stood and wiped his hands on the ever-present rag slung through the belt loop of his jeans and set about preparing her order. A customer approached the bar and sat down. "I'll be with you in a—" He blinked. "Lydia. Hi."

Back stiff, head held high, she fit in to the bar scene about as well as the Pope at a Victoria's Secret fashion show.

She sort of smiled at him and nodded.

"I'll be with you in just a sec," he told her, hurrying to fill Edwina's drink order.

When he returned to Lydia, she reminded him of the way she'd looked when he'd first met her—uptight and unapproachable. She wore a navy-blue suit this time, only slightly less conservative than the gray one, minus the dryer sheet. Now, instead of thinking her unfriendly, he understood she was just out of her element.

"This is a surprise," he said, grinning.

She adjusted her position on the tall barstool and lifted her chin a notch. "I have a favor to ask."

He spread his hands. "Ask away."

She leaned forward and motioned for him to do the same, obviously not wanting her words to be overheard by anyone, not that anyone was within hearing range. "You mentioned the other day that you could introduce me to some men here," she said. "I mean *man*, singular. One man. I don't need more than one. So if the offer still stands..."

"Absolutely, but..." He frowned. "You're not looking for a, ah, gay man anymore?"

Lydia jerked and sat up straighter, glancing around with narrowed eyes. "This isn't a gay bar?" she whispered.

New compassion swept over him for her predicament, realizing how hard it must have been for her to come down here and ask this favor of him. He wished he could lie to her. "No. It's not."

Her cheeks deepened in color as she pushed away from the bar. "Okay. Good-bye."

He grabbed her wrist, stopping her from leaving. "Wait a sec. Don't go just yet, okay?" He glanced down the bar toward Edwina, who sipped her Coke, her hip resting against the counter as she watched them. "Hey, Edwina?" One of her eyebrows lifted in response. "Could you hold down the fort for a few minutes?"

She chewed her gum and blew a bubble, looking back and forth between him and Lydia over the top of the expanding pink orb. She popped the gum and jerked her head in a semblance of a nod, her long, dark hair swaying with the movement.

* * * *

With a firm hand against her upper back, Mitch propelled Lydia out of the bar and out the door. She peered back through the windows and could just make out that waitress standing behind the bar and staring out at them.

"She's beautiful," she said, turning back to Mitch. Something about that woman signaled a déjà vu of sorts in her mind, but she couldn't quite put a finger on it.

"Who? Edwina?" He glanced into the pub. "Yeah, she is."

Edwina's showstopping figure and stunning looks caused Lydia to self-consciously smooth back her boring, pulled-tight-into-a-bun-as-usual hair. She couldn't imagine a woman like Edwina ever advertising in the gay personals. She couldn't imagine Edwina making a boob of herself by assuming Mitch worked at a gay bar.

With the heel of her palm, she bonked herself in the side of the head a few times. "Just shoot me, will you?"

Mitch pulled her hand away from her head. "You're too hard on yourself, Lydia."

For a moment she zeroed in on the feeling of his large, warm hand holding hers. It felt good, like it belonged there, which was a crazy thought. Reality returned, and she pulled her hand from his grasp.

"What in the world was I thinking?" she asked. Her skin burned from embarrassment, or the heat of summer, or his touch…or all the above.

"It's understandable you'd assume I worked at a gay bar. I mean, you think I…er…"

She waved her hand back and forth. "No, no. That was just plain stupidity. What I meant was, I had this grand notion of you helping me out and transforming me into the belle of the ball. You know, *Queer Eye* my style or something." She wrapped her arms around herself despite the warm air and strode down the alley. If a sinkhole opened up in front of her, she'd gladly fall into it.

He jogged up beside her as they reached the sidewalk. "I don't know about the clothing and hair stuff," he said, "but I could certainly give you advice on men." He cleared his throat and coughed. "I mean, since I'm a, ah, man."

"That's okay. It was a dumb idea. Besides, I don't want advice on men. It would be pointless." She pulled black-framed sunglasses from her purse and exchanged them for her regular glasses to block the blinding glare off the sidewalk.

Mitch didn't respond right away, so she knew he silently agreed with her. Finally, he asked, "Why would it be pointless?"

She had about a million reasons. "It just would be."

"Why?" he persisted.

"Because."

"You remind me of my kid brothers and sisters growing up. Whenever I'd ask them why they did or didn't do something, they'd always say the same thing, 'because.'"

"You're comparing me to a child?" She figured she should be annoyed, but she was sort of amused.

She felt his eyes on her and turned her head to see him appraising her from head to toe. For some ridiculous reason, the trail of his gaze heated her skin.

"No," he said. "I'm definitely not comparing you to a child." He grinned, and his white teeth flashed in the sunlight, blinding her. "I'm just poking fun at you. You need to lighten up."

"Thanks, Dad."

He elbowed her in the arm, jostling her aside and making her almost stumble. "Tell me *why* it's pointless."

His flirtatious manner flustered her. She smoothed the hair off her face. So this particular drop-dead gorgeous man just happened to be gay, which meant he wasn't exactly flirting. "Uh, do you come from a big family, Mitch?"

He nudged her again. "You're changing the subject."

"How many brothers and sisters?"

"Three sisters and three brothers. Why is it pointless, Lydia?" he asked without missing a beat.

"Well, for one, I wouldn't know how to act. Are they younger or older, and do they live around here?"

It was his turn to try to follow her line of questioning. "Oh, I see how it's going to be. All younger, and they live in Nevada, where I grew up, except for a sister who lives in Seattle. Why wouldn't you know how to act?"

"Because it's been forever since I was on a date. So you're the eldest child of seven. What was it like growing up in such a large family?"

They turned a corner and strolled into the same square they'd met in at Alive After Five two days ago, but now the area was mostly vacant.

"Crazy. Hectic." He laughed as if remembering the good times. "Let's just say I relish my free time these days."

She smiled, her heart filled with envy. "I can't imagine growing up with brothers and sisters."

"You're an only child?"

"Yeah. Just me." She sighed. "Someday I'd love a big family of my own. Of course, I'd need a husband to do that, and it's kind of hard to get a husband when you don't date."

They found an empty bench and sat. A couple of young men dressed in ratty jeans hanging low on bony hips played Frisbee in front of them. Lydia watched awhile without really seeing them, mentally counting off how many inches separated her from Mitch, which was ridiculous because he was gay, and she shouldn't be thinking about such things with him. She forced herself to mentally chill.

Mitch's arm rested on the back of the bench. If she was to scoot maybe two, three inches, the tips of his fingers would brush her shoulder. The thought made her skin tingle. She realized he was watching her.

She turned and met his gaze. His eyes smiled, and a grin tugged at his lips. "Do you realize you've gotten me totally off course in this conversation?" he asked.

"That was my hope."

"Why don't you date, Lydia?" His expression turned serious.

"Basically, because I don't have time."

He studied her, and his fingers drummed silently on the back of the bench. Again, she felt the odd tingle in her shoulder.

"You don't like to talk much about yourself, do you?"

She shrugged. "There's nothing interesting to talk about."

"I seriously doubt that." A strange light shone in his eyes, his expression so earnest she dropped her gaze.

"It's true. My life revolves around my job and my dad. There's no time for anything else."

"Your dad?"

She nodded. "He was in a car accident a few years back and suffered a serious head injury. Although he's made a lot of progress, he can't care for himself. I live with him and take care of him. I'm sure you can imagine that doesn't go over well with prospective suitors." She twisted her shoe against the red bricks and concentrated on that scraping sound for a moment. "It's like a single mom trying to get a date. Once a guy learns of our responsibilities, they can't find the door fast enough."

She glanced up at Mitch in time to see embarrassment sweep across his face. She pointed a finger at him. "I rest my case."

"What?" He still looked guilty, but to his credit, he didn't try to defend his stance. Apparently, single gay men weren't all that different from single straight men.

"Not all men are that shallow," he said.

"The men I know are."

He cleared his throat. "So when was the last time you went on a date?"

She gave him her best stern expression. "What is this, twenty questions?"

Unfazed, he said, "Yes. Curiosity is part of my job description. Get used to it. So?"

She shifted so that her knees pointed away from him on the bench. She didn't have to answer that. It was none of his business. "That's right. You're a writer, too."

"Yes. Don't change the subject, Lydia."

She tried her best to glare at him for being so presumptuous, but it was impossible. His warm brown eyes lured her closed-off side out from behind the wall she usually had built around herself. He was just so darn easy to talk to.

She sighed and leaned back on the bench, her spine pressing somewhat uncomfortably against the hard wood. "Well, I moved back to Boise five years ago, and guys haven't exactly been lining up at my door since then. Like I said, I don't think I'd even know how to act around a man anymore." Not that she ever really had.

Mitch nudged her arm. "You act just fine with me."

"You don't count," she said.

He chuckled, replacing his arm on the backrest. "Thanks a lot."

She leaned over and slapped him lightly in the ribs. "You know what I mean." An ant crawled over the shoe of her outstretched foot. When it moved onto her stocking, she bent down and gently flicked it off. It scurried away and disappeared into a crack on a nearby brick.

"So that's my life, or lack thereof, in a nutshell. My dating experience could fit on the head of a pin, with room left over to stretch my arms."

Mitch jumped to his feet and held out his hand. She eyed it, but didn't take it. "Come back to the bar with me," he said.

She shook her head. "Oh no."

He pulled her to her feet until she stood right in front of him. She met his brown eyes then dropped her gaze to his broad chest. That view was more than pleasant, but it brought an unwelcome tingle to certain intimate areas of her body that had no business tingling, considering Mitch was gay. She stepped backward and focused on those grungy Frisbee players. They were a neutral view for her whacked-out hormones.

"You came down here today with a mission, didn't you?" he asked. "I know it must have taken a lot of guts to do that, right?"

He didn't know how much. Her guts felt completely wrung out. She was afraid to nod, wondering where he was going with this.

"Like I said before, we get quite a few decent guys in the pub and—"

"Mitch," she said wearily, "I wouldn't know a decent guy from an indecent one. I wouldn't know when a guy is sincere or when he's feeding me a line."

He grinned and nodded. "That's what I'm getting at. If you come in while I'm working, I can help you out. You know, give you, ah, pointers on the guys who approach you."

"Kind of like dating lessons?"

"Dating *tips*. Advice about men." He grinned again.

Lydia worried her lower lip. Was there even a point in trying to meet someone? What if she actually met someone she liked? Once he learned about her dad...

"Stop that, Lydia."

"What?"

"You're thinking of every single reason why this won't work. I can see all the excuses churning in your head."

She studied him through narrowed eyes. "Why are you willing to do this for me?"

"Because I like you and because you asked for my help. Remember?"

She blushed.

"Besides, there was a time when my life was out of control, too. When my responsibilities left time for little else. I remember how resentful and angry I was."

"I'm not resentful and angry."

Instead of responding to that, he nudged her playfully in her shoulder. "Come on. Whatta you say? Your one-night prince could very well be in the pub as we speak."

Chapter 3

Lydia lagged behind as they approached the door of The Alley, wondering about her sanity, or lack thereof. First, she advertised for a gay escort to her reunion, and now she'd asked a gay man to teach her the finer points of meeting men.

Somebody call Oprah.

She barely glanced at Mitch as he held the oak-and-glass door open for her, and used tunnel vision as she followed him between the sparsely populated tables until they reached the bar. That voluptuous, dark-haired waitress—Edwina, wasn't it?—acknowledged them with a slight nod of her head from across the room.

Lydia slid onto one of the high barstools, a quick look to her right and left assuring her that most of the others stools were empty, thank goodness. She reached for a handful of peanuts to occupy her hands.

Mitch rounded the bar and stepped in front of her. "What can I get you?"

She finished chewing the nuts. "How about a glass of Chardonnay?"

His brows furrowed. "I thought you said you don't drink."

"That was an excuse."

He watched her a moment. "Lesson number one. Honesty is the best policy."

"This coming from a man?"

He made a face at her. "Rather than making up some excuse why you can't go out with a guy—like telling me you didn't drink to avoid having drinks with me—tell him the truth, that you're just not interested. Otherwise, he's going to keep bugging you."

That made sense, she supposed. Honesty was a good thing.

He poured a glass of wine and handed it to her, resting his elbows on the shiny wood. "Don't worry, m'dear. Tonight's lesson—number two, I believe—is an easy one."

"Oh, you've developed a lesson plan, have you? I'm impressed."

"As well you should be. All you have to do is drink your wine."

"That's it? *That's* the lesson? Thank God I'm not paying for this course, or I'd be demanding my money back."

He chuckled. "That's enough, Miss Wisecracker. The reason for this simple lesson is to get you used to being here."

He rapped a knuckle on the gleaming counter and turned to help another customer. As he walked off, she tried not to admire the scrumptious way his Levi's fit his lower body. "You are pathetic," she muttered to herself, forcing her gaze away.

Feeling a bit more relaxed after a few sips of wine, she glanced in Mitch's direction. He and the customer with him looked her way. When the other man smiled at her, her face heated up, and she turned, shifting her position to stare straight ahead at the rows of liquor bottles on the shelves. The mirrored wall behind them reflected her flushed face, so she refocused her gaze on her wineglass instead.

A few minutes later, Mitch rejoined her, a rag slung over the shoulder of his button-down burgundy shirt. "Ouch."

"What?"

"If looks could kill, that guy over there would be dead."

She'd hoped it wasn't so obvious.

"You glared at him, Lydia. Then you turned very pointedly away."

"It was just a turn."

"No, it was a total brush-off."

"Really? What should I have done? I don't want him to think I'm available."

Mitch's loud laugh caused a nearby table of customers to glance their way. His voice quieter, he said, "You *are* available, Lydia.

That's why you're here."

"But–but I don't want him to get the wrong impression."

"What wrong impression? That you won't bite his head off if he came over and said hello?"

Lydia blushed, knowing he was right. "I guess I flunked that lesson, didn't I?"

He grabbed the white rag from his shoulder and flicked her in the arm. "Don't worry. I grade on a curve."

* * * *

Lydia spent much of the weekend recounting what a dork she'd been on her first night of "lessons" with Mitch. If it wasn't for the reunion just a few weeks away, she'd call him and tell him she'd changed her mind. As it was, she'd promised to stop by the pub one night this week.

Monday evening, as she returned home after a long day in the law library, scattered rain showers broke through the heat, making the air muggy and sticky. The unseasonably foul weather matched her anxious mood as she paused with her hand on the back door of her house.

She lifted her gaze to the sky and said a silent prayer. Opening the door and stepping across the threshold, she saw immediately her prayer had not been answered.

Today's caregiver wore a short, spiky hairstyle, the black hair encircling a stern expression on pale skin. She reminded Lydia of a black beetle with pinchers.

"How did everything go?" Lydia held her breath.

"We have a problem," the beetle replied. "You didn't tell us he required so much hands-on care and attention."

Lydia blinked at the woman's sharp tone of voice and wondered who "us" referred to. "I was very up front on the phone. I told you specifically that—"

The woman continued as if Lydia hadn't spoken. "He simply wore us out with all his demands."

Lydia realized the woman referred to herself in plural, as in more than one beetle. Get out the Raid.

"We will not be able to continue without a significant increase in our fees."

Lydia's heart sank. She couldn't afford to pay much more. "How significant?" She crossed to the refrigerator and pulled out a bottled water then unscrewed the lid and took a long swig.

"We'll have to get back to you on that." Beetle woman turned sharply and exited the house.

Lydia stared after the closed door a few moments, alternately feeling like throwing something and crying. She'd taken care of her dad for years without help, and this woman, this *professional*, couldn't handle him?

* * * *

The wind whipped Mitch's hair as his Harley rumbled along Highway 21 outside of Boise. There was nothing like a long ride on his baby to clear his mind. Today, it wasn't working. He'd started the ride feeling like an ass. He'd been riding for more than an hour and still felt like an ass.

He had to tell Lydia the truth. He wanted to continue helping her if she'd let him, but he couldn't go on with her thinking he was gay. He and Lydia barely knew each other, but he enjoyed the easiness between them. He liked being around her, and she seemed to trust him. Yet this burgeoning friendship was all based on a lie. Had he known he'd see her again after that first meeting, he'd never have gone along with the gay thing.

Now it was out there, and he had to get it back.

Mitch slowed the big bike as he cruised down Harrison Boulevard, reading the street names. Finding the right one, he signaled and turned into it. Homes from another era passed him on either side of the tree-lined street.

The sound of the Harley's engine broke the serenity of the peaceful neighborhood, yet Mitch liked it that way. It made him feel like a manly man, a feeling he'd need in the coming minutes when he told Lydia the truth.

He scanned the houses for the correct address. Finding it, he slid the bike to a stop and cut the engine. He swung his leg over the seat then strolled up the sidewalk to the large gray house. A wraparound porch spanned the entire front of the first floor like a moat, and a weather-worn picket fence enclosed the yard. The place even had a turret, and he wondered if that was Lydia's room. The tower bedroom. Like Cinderella.

He could never live in a place like this. With the fences and railings and dark colors, it was too claustrophobic. He'd take his simple house in the hills any day of the week, with its modern lines and sleek interior.

He pushed open the gate and walked halfway up the sidewalk before he realized someone watched him from the porch. An elderly man sat guard in a wheelchair, staring at Mitch with steely eyes. Mitch put on a big smile and bounded up the steps, onto the veranda.

Whipping off his mirror-lens sunglasses, he said, "Hi there. You must be Lydia's dad." He stuck out his hand.

The old man continued to stare, not even glancing at the proffered greeting.

Mitch pulled back somewhat awkwardly and brushed his fingers through his hair, trying to remember what Lydia had said about her dad's condition. A brain injury, he recalled. She'd mentioned him having good days and bad days. Apparently, this was a bad day.

"I'm Mitch Gannon. I was wondering if, ah, Lydia was around." *Yes, of course she's around, you idiot.* Like she'd really go off and leave her father at home alone. That would be a new take on the old *Home Alone* series, wouldn't it? *Home Alone: The Senior Years.*

Again, the man said nothing.

"O-kay," Mitch said with false cheerfulness. "I'm just going to knock on the door and see if she answers."

Lydia answered within seconds of the first knock, and a waft of yummy food smells drifted outside. Her pretty blue eyes behind the gold-wire frames were worried, startled, and flustered all at the same time when she saw him.

"Mitch," she gasped through the screen, her voice breathy. "I thought you were—What are you doing here?"

She'd gathered her blonde hair into a high ponytail, the end disappearing behind her shoulders. He had the crazy urge to spin her around so he could see just where it stopped.

"I was—" He'd been about to say he was just in the neighborhood, but who'd believe he was riding his Harley around the historical homes of North End Boise? He cleared his throat. "I came by to see you."

She searched his face, her expression wary. Then a smile curved her mouth as she pushed open the screen door and stepped onto the porch. "You're so sweet."

Mitch shifted his position, his worn riding boots scuffing against the planked veranda. He wasn't so sweet. He was a jerk.

She looked past him. "Is that yours?"

He turned and saw she referred to the Harley. "Yup. That's my baby. I bought her the same day I moved to Boise and bought my freedom. She's a beaut, isn't she?"

Lydia nodded and moved to the railing, her hands gripping the wood as she stared out at the road. The tip of her ponytail brushed her shoulder blades. He wondered what it would look like long and flowing across her shoulders. He swept his gaze down her body, startled to realize she had a very nice shape. Released from the captivity of conservative- and shapeless-suit hell, her figure was very nice indeed.

More than nice, he thought as his eyes traveled down to her

backside, where her faded jeans hugged her trim bottom. She might not have much in the breast department, but the rest of her was just right. His groin flexed. His body apparently didn't realize he was supposed to be gay.

She turned back to him a split second after his eyes had been on her ass. "Did you meet my dad?"

His mind still on the aforementioned body part, he was slow to respond. Finally, he glanced her father's way. The man sat in the same position with the same expression. "I, uh, introduced myself, but he didn't seem to hear me."

She made a face. "Oh, he heard you just fine. He must be mad about something again. Although *I* should be the one who's mad today," she said in a slightly louder voice, obviously wanting her dad to hear. "He scared away another caregiver today. I swear he's worse than a child sometimes." With a look of pure exasperation, she clasped a hand over Mitch's forearm and led him in front of the wheelchair.

She squatted to the old man's level. "Dad?" she said, peering up at him.

Even though she'd said she was angry at her father, love shone in her eyes, bringing a warm feeling to the pit of Mitch's belly, along with a twinge of shame. He'd spent the better part of his childhood taking care of his younger siblings while his parents took care of themselves. Those years had definitely worn on him. He'd had a hard time with any semblance of patience and outward show of affection after a time. Lydia, obviously, didn't suffer from the same selfishness.

"Dad, I want you to meet someone." She motioned for Mitch to squat beside her. "This is Mitch Gannon. Mitch, this is my father, Robert St. Clair."

Clear blue eyes in an otherwise passive face focused on Mitch. Something unintelligible that sounded awfully close to a swear word spat from the wrinkled mouth.

Mitch glanced sidelong at Lydia, who had turned away, but a

crimson blush swept up her neck. She patted her dad's leg and stood up.

"I'm sorry," she whispered in his ear when he stood, her warm breath fanning his earlobe.

He touched her arm in a show of empathy as they took several steps away from the wheelchair. "Hey. Anyone who's been through what he's been through can say whatever he wants."

"But it was rude."

He shrugged. "I've been called worse."

She met his gaze and smiled, showing her teeth. How had he ever thought she was anything but lovely?

Rising on tiptoe, she kissed his cheek, her breath whispering across his lips as she pulled away. With an inward sigh of regret, he knew for a fact she wouldn't do that if she realized he was straight.

She tipped her head toward her father. "Would you mind keeping him company for a minute? I have something on the stove. In fact, if you don't have dinner plans, why don't you stay? I'll warn you, though, it's nothing fancy."

Mitch hesitated, certain she wouldn't be so eager for his company once she learned the truth. By staying, he would have more opportunity to tell her. "That sounds great. I'm a terrible cook myself, so it's not often I get a home-cooked meal."

"Maybe I'll give you cooking lessons sometime. You know, quid pro quo."

Cooking lessons didn't sound all that thrilling, but cooking lessons with Lydia might be more than pleasant. Unfortunately, that day would never come, not after tonight.

She smiled at him and disappeared into the house, her swaying hips a beacon to his eyes. He plopped down onto the top porch step, not far from the wheels of the old man's chair.

"How much...she offering you?" The words were slow and deliberate but otherwise clear.

Mitch furrowed his brows and turned to Lydia's dad. "What?"

Another quiet string of expletives, this one a bit more colorful. He seemed to have no problem getting *those* words out. "Whatever it…is, it won't be enough. You'll quit before the end of your…first week."

"Quitting?" Mitch scooted closer. "I'm sorry, sir, but I have no idea what you're talking about."

A UPS truck pulled in behind the Harley. Mitch glanced protectively toward his bike then turned back to the old man.

Clear, intelligent eyes assessed him. "My daughter didn't hire you to be my…babysitter?" The last slowly drawn-out word dripped with derision.

Mitch couldn't help chuckling. It was as far-fetched as the idea of him being gay. "Hell no. Lydia and I are friends."

From the corner of his eye, Mitch saw the UPS guy stride briskly up the sidewalk toward the house. He started to rise to intercept him when Robert St. Clair pressed a button, and his wheelchair rammed into Mitch's thigh.

"Ouch," he muttered, rubbing the side of his leg.

"You…sleepin' with her?"

Both the UPS guy and Mitch heard that shouted question, and damn if Mitch didn't blush like a schoolgirl. "Er, no."

"Why the hell not?"

"Well, uh, er—" he stammered, one of the rare times he'd been speechless in his life. The UPS guy stood at the bottom step, taking it all in, waiting for someone to look his way.

"He's gay, Dad."

All three men swiveled their heads as Lydia stepped onto the porch.

"What?" the old man yelled, as if suddenly deaf.

"Mitch is gay," she shouted back, her voice several octaves louder than necessary.

The UPS guy practically dropped his package, Robert St. Clair harrumphed under his breath, and damn if Mitch didn't feel that flush creeping up his neck again.

Now, he had nothing against gay people, but he certainly didn't enjoy hearing the words "Mitch is gay" shouted from the rooftops of Boise. Especially not in front of a young Joe Stud like the UPS guy here, and even more especially not on the day he planned on setting Lydia straight. It took every ounce of willpower he had not to blurt out the truth then and there.

After several moments of awkward silence that felt like forever, the UPS guy cleared his throat. "I, uh, need a signature for this package." His gaze landed on Lydia, and he checked her out head to toe.

Mitch figured most women would go gaga over someone like Joe Stud here. The guy was tall, tan, and built.

Lydia didn't seem to notice. The epitome of primness and propriety, she set down the tray of lemonade and snatched the clipboard away. Without even making eye contact with him, she scrawled out her signature and exchanged the clipboard for the package. "Thank you," she said.

A few minutes later, the UPS truck pulled away from the curb. Robert St. Clair stared at Mitch for many long, uncomfortable moments. Finally, he rotated his wheelchair to face Lydia and said in clear and unwavering voice, "This boy is no more gay than my name is Elvis Presley."

* * * *

Mitch stared at the ground for countless seconds. Robert drummed his gnarled fingers against the handles of the wheelchair, and Lydia wanted to crawl into a hole and disappear.

Instead, she watched until the brown truck turned the corner down the street. Then she cleared her throat.

Mitch glanced her way at the sound.

"I'm sorry," she mouthed, nodding her head toward her dad. Relief flooded her when Mitch grinned that endearing grin that would make her heart swoon if she let it. Which of course, she wouldn't.

"It's okay," he mouthed back, and Lydia wanted to hug him. Her dad alienated just about everyone, but Mitch seemed to shrug off her dad's rudeness like water off a duck's feathers.

She grabbed a lemonade from the tray she'd brought out and set it in a cupholder attached to the wheelchair. Then she handed a glass to Mitch.

While he drank, she took a moment to stare at him unfettered, something she'd tried not to do since she'd first opened the door tonight. The sight of him standing on her front porch had been enough to make her nerves skitter up her spine like ants at a picnic.

His white T-shirt stretched taut over his torso and broad shoulders, the dark-blue and silver Seattle Mariners logo covering what she could only imagine was a rock-hard stomach and well-defined chest. If she was to risk peeking, she knew his lower body would look just as sumptuous in those faded jeans. *He's gay. He's gay. He's gay.* She tightened her ponytail at its base then shoved her hands into her jeans pockets.

Raising her gaze to Mitch's face, she saw him watching her, which meant he'd probably caught her entire appraisal of his body. She blushed and pulled her hands from her pockets, crossing her arms over her chest.

"Lydia." He said her name softly, like a caress. The minute that thought entered her mind, she reprimanded herself. He'd simply said her name, no big deal. It wasn't a caress but a rebuke for looking at him the way she had. So why had her pulse sped up like a runaway train? *Idiot, idiot, idiot.*

Some emotion she couldn't decipher crossed his expression. Then he cocked his head toward the house. "Can we talk?" He motioned to her dad. "Alone?"

She pulled open the screen door and let him pass into the foyer, his musky male scent entering the house with him. She inhaled deeply.

Once inside, he turned to her. "Lydia—"

Knowing what was coming, she blurted out, "I'm so sorry, Mitch. You told me the other day that you didn't want people to know about your...lifestyle, and here I go shouting it out to the whole neighborhood."

* * * *

Lydia's dinner tasted fabulous, but Mitch feared the pleasant meal she'd prepared had been a waste of time. Robert St. Clair barely touched the pasta dish, slapping Lydia's hand away as if it were an annoying fly every time she tried to help him eat. He spent almost the entire meal time glaring at Mitch, which naturally made it difficult for Mitch to enjoy his meal.

Lydia wasn't oblivious to the tension and tried to alleviate the strain. "Dad, you and Mitch have something in common. Mitch is a writer, too." She turned to Mitch. "Dad used to write all the time. Primarily speech writing, but his passion was screenplays. In fact, he even produced a couple of his plays at local theaters, didn't you, Dad?"

Robert glared at Mitch.

Lydia's cheeks flamed red. To Mitch she said, "You didn't tell me what kind of writing you do."

Glad to focus on something other than the old man's evil eye, Mitch said, "I write mysteries."

Her eyes lit up. "Really? Are—"

"No, I'm not published yet." He forced a grin, used to the question. Most people, when they heard he was unpublished, commented on his nice "hobby," then changed the subject. It always annoyed him.

"Oh. But what I was asking was, are you writing a whodunit or a thriller type of mystery?"

Of course she wouldn't respond like everyone else. Lydia St. Clair was clearly not like everyone else. "I write the old-fashioned private-eye mystery. My guy is an amateur who just happened to fall into detective work. Sort of a bumbling hero." He grinned, thinking of his character.

Lydia rested her chin in her hands. "Have you always wanted to write?"

"Since I was a kid."

"Have you ever submitted anything?"

He nodded. "You could probably wallpaper your kitchen with all my rejection letters."

She wrinkled up her nose into a cute, sympathetic expression that had him aching to lean across the table and kiss her. "That's got to be tough."

He shrugged. "You sort of get used to—" His water glass tipped over, spilling liquid onto his plate. He hurried to right the glass. "Whoops, sorry. I don't know how that happened."

She stared at her father. "Dad. Why'd you do that?"

Mitch glanced at Robert, surprised.

"I want to go…for a walk."

Lydia continued to stare at him for a long moment. Then she sighed. "Okay. I guess the dishes can wait." She started to push away from the table.

"No!" Robert slammed the table with his fist, causing both Mitch and Lydia to jump back in their chairs. "Mitch will…take me. You stay. Dishes."

Mitch looked back and forth between father and daughter, curious as to Lydia's reaction. Himself, he'd tell the old man to jump in a lake at the order, but she just nodded resignedly.

A few minutes later, Mitch pushed the wheelchair down the ramp behind the house. Lydia stood behind him in the doorway of the kitchen.

"Why don't you wait on the dishes?" he asked. "I'll help when we get back."

She shooed her hand at him. "Don't worry about it. There isn't much to do." She motioned down the street. "There's a nice park that way with plenty of shade. Dad likes to watch the kids and talk about how much better behaved children were in his day."

Robert harrumphed under his breath. Mitch waved good-bye to Lydia and headed down the sidewalk, wondering what the old man was up to. He had a bad feeling it was about more than getting some fresh air.

They'd walked the span of several houses before Robert spoke. "So what's all this…nonsense about you being…gay?"

There it was. "What do you mean?" he answered, purposefully vague.

"Stop walking…Come around here."

Mitch slowed the wheelchair.

"Down here." Robert reached for Mitch's arm, bony fingers curling around his wrist and tugging downward.

Mitch squatted until they were at face level with each other.

"My cousin Louis on my mother's side was a homo…sexual. Talked with a lisp…limp wrist…whole shebang. We used to take him out…behind woodshed…beat the crap out of him."

Oh, great. Lydia's dad was a closet bigot. "Uh, with all due respect, sir, times have changed and—"

Robert shushed him. "We didn't…beat him up because he…was gay, but because…he was a sniveling idiot."

Mitch's brows lifted. He could remember a few of those himself growing up. He stopped smirking when he saw the way Robert stared at him. "Sir?"

"Don't…sssir me. Tell…truth."

"About…?" He played dumb. It was safer.

The wheelchair rammed into his knee. Apparently dumb wasn't so safe. A part of him wanted to lie again, but a bigger part wanted at least one of the three people in this world who thought he was gay to know the truth. The UPS guy would, alas, probably never be enlightened. Besides, Mr. St. Clair might have an idea on how to set Lydia straight, so to speak.

Rubbing his knee with one hand, Mitch said, "You were right about what you said earlier, sir. You're no Elvis Presley, and I'm…as straight as the rails on that fence over there." Both men turned to look at the white picket fence running beside the sidewalk across the street. A giant weight lifted from his shoulders.

"Why does my…daughter think you're gay?"

"It's a long story." He stood and moved behind the wheelchair, gripping the handles.

"I'm listening."

With a loud exhale, Mitch explained everything as they headed toward the park Lydia had mentioned. When he finished, he said, "I haven't been truthful with your daughter, and I'm really sorry about that. I'll tell her the truth the minute we get back. You have my—"

The wheelchair came to such a sudden stop he practically fell on top of the old man. Robert had obviously used the hand brakes.

"You'll do no such…thing, young man."

Confused, Mitch circled the chair and squatted to Robert's level again, this time ensuring his knees were nowhere near the wheels. "You don't want me to tell her the truth? Why not?" Maybe Lydia's dad wasn't all together in the mental department. Either that, or Mitch wasn't. Either scenario was entirely possible.

"My daughter…never dates. Partly because of me. And partly because she…" He took a long breath and appeared to build up more energy to continue speaking. "You saw how she was with…that delivery boy. She's very shy with men. Had…some bad experiences."

"Sir," Mitch said, placing a hand on Robert's arm, uncomfortable with the personal turn of conversation. He didn't want to hear details about Lydia's private life unless she did the telling.

Robert waved off Mitch's unease then plopped his hand down in his thin lap. "She likes you, Mitch. I may be old and half-baked, but…not blind."

"She thinks I'm gay."

Robert nodded. "Which is why she's let herself become friendly…with you." He shot him with a direct stare. "You know that."

Mitch stared at the sidewalk and nodded.

"If she learns you're…not gay…friends no more." His shaking hand touched Mitch's sleeve. "You know that, too."

Again, Mitch nodded. Yes, he knew that, too. "But that's a chance I need to take. I—"

Robert's thin fingers curled around Mitch's wrist. "Please. Don't tell her. At least not yet. I'm not a well man, and it does my heart good to see my girl have…a life other than me for a change." He clutched at his chest, his breathing labored. "Please. For me," he whispered in a scratchy voice.

Mitch stared hard at Robert a few moments then sighed. "Okay." He rose and stepped behind the chair, not liking what he'd just agreed to but also not wanting to drive the old man into a coronary. "But just for now."

Chapter 4

"My dad says hi," Lydia told Mitch a few nights later at the pub. "He seems to really like you, which is amazing because he doesn't like anyone. Sometimes I even wonder if he likes me."

Mitch flashed her a smile and wiped a water ring from the counter. "It's my charming personality," he said.

She sipped her Chardonnay and shook her head. "No, that's not it."

"Gee, thanks." He flicked her with the wet towel.

She rubbed the damp spot from her sleeve. "Seriously. He's rude to or ignores practically everyone he meets—he's especially hard on his poor sitters, as I've told you. The only people he's even *remotely* nice to are my friends. I suppose that's why he likes you."

For the first time since she'd started coming into The Alley, she smiled. Not a huge smile, just a slight lift of her lips, enough to draw his attention to her mouth. She had full pink lips that looked soft and—Christ. He didn't think of her in a romantic way, so why did he have the sudden urge to learn just how soft and kissable those lips were?

This being gay thing was really becoming a royal pain.

"Ready for your lesson?" he asked, his voice squawking like a hormonal pubescent.

"Yes, teacher." She batted her eyelashes at him. "Will there be homework this time?"

Several examples of sensual homework leapt unexpectedly into his mind—most involved getting her naked. What the hell was wrong with him? He pushed his dirty thoughts aside long enough to get out a coherent sentence. "No homework, my dear pupil. Today's lesson is also very simple. You need to pay attention."

"You going to get out the ruler and rap my knuckles next? I *am* paying attention."

He shook his head, grinning. "I meant pay attention to your surroundings. If a man smiles at you, I want you to notice and to smile back."

A faint blush colored her cheeks. "You must think I'm pretty pathetic that I have to be told to even smile at a guy."

He placed the palms of his hands flat on the counter and leaned close to her. "If you use the term 'pathetic' to describe yourself one more time, I'll have to take you over my knee and spank you. Got it?"

"Ooh, I'm scared now." She waved her hands and wiggled her fingers as if casting a spell on him, which maybe she was because now he pictured her bent over his lap with her shapely bare ass under his hand as he—

He was the pathetic one here, not her.

"So who's the girlfriend?" Edwina asked a few minutes later as he handed her a tray of drinks.

"Lydia's just a friend."

"You seem awfully chummy with her."

"You seem jealous."

She rolled her dark eyes. "Get over yourself." She nodded her head toward Lydia. "She's not your type."

As he watched, Lydia rifled through her purse, pretty much ignoring her surroundings. She pulled out a tube of lipstick and a compact. Nudging her glasses down her nose, she stared over the frames into the small mirror as she touched the pink tip of the lipstick to her full bottom lip.

"Like I just said, she and I are…" His voice trailed off as Lydia applied the color. What on earth was wrong with him? It wasn't like he'd never seen a woman apply lipstick before, for Christ's sake! So what that he'd never noticed lipsticks were phallus shaped?

"Earth to Gannon." Edwina waved her hand in front of his face, snapping her fingers a few times. Her gaze narrowed as she stared at him. Without another word, she turned and flounced off. Mitch headed the opposite direction, toward Lydia, mentally screwing his head on straight.

She leaned across the bar as he approached. Thinking she wanted to tell him something, he rested his elbows on the counter and leaned toward her. When she puckered her lips into a kiss, one of his elbows slipped on the polished mahogany surface, slamming his shoulder into the counter.

Thankfully, Lydia ignored the dumbass move and beckoned him closer, closer—

"Is this a good color for me?"

He blinked. "Huh?" was about all he could manage as he stared at her lips.

"The lipstick. I just bought it. Is it a good color for me?"

He blinked again, still not fully comprehending what she had asked.

A slap on the arm brought him quickly back to reality. "Jeez, Gannon. What is your problem?" Edwina reached her hand across the bar. "Hi, I'm Edwina. Neanderthal boy here hasn't a clue either. Let me see."

Looking back and forth between Mitch and Edwina, Lydia pressed her lips together in a nervous movement then lifted her chin slightly, pushing her glasses back into place.

Edwina squinted and cocked her head to the side. "It's a pretty color, but it doesn't go with your skin tone. I think you need something with an orangey base."

Skin tone? Orangey base? Mitch scratched his temple. Where did women learn these things? He circled his shoulder a couple of times to get the kinks out.

Lydia reached into her purse and pulled out another tube. "This is the only other one I have." She opened it up, and there came that phallic shape again, this time bright red. Mitch nearly groaned. If she touched it to her mouth again, he would need a cold shower.

Edwina squinted at it. "Probably not your color, but try it anyway."

Lydia wiped off her current lipstick with a napkin and applied the new color. Despite Edwina's comment, it looked perfectly good to Mitch. In fact, her lips looked so good his jeans tightened at the crotch.

She blotted the lipstick with a napkin and set it down on the counter. A perfect and sexy red imprint of her lips stared up at him. His pants tightened to the point of discomfort.

"I gotta—" He waved his hand toward the other end of the bar. "Busy. Customers. I really have to—" He spun on his heel and headed toward the far end of the counter, away from Lydia and her lips.

* * * *

"That's weird," Edwina said, staring after him, her eyes narrowed.

"What?" Lydia asked, peering one more time into the compact mirror before snapping it shut. She liked this color even if Edwina didn't.

Edwina looked back at her. "So what's with you and Gannon?"

"What do you mean?" Lydia had never been good at reading people, but the little green monster glowed bright and clear on this beautiful woman's face.

The realization was so ridiculous on several levels she almost burst out laughing, but Edwina didn't look amused. If Mitch *was* straight, he certainly wouldn't choose her over Edwina, who was about the sexiest woman she'd ever met.

She remembered Mitch had told her no one at the bar knew about his lifestyle and that he wanted to keep it that way. She swallowed back her giggle and cleared her throat. "Mitch and I are just friends. Nothing more."

Edwina stared at her awhile as if trying to read her face and ascertain the truth of her words. Finally, her expression relaxed into a slight smile, and she nodded. "So why ask his opinion on lipstick?"

Lydia's cheeks warmed. "Well…" She puzzled over an answer that wouldn't betray Mitch.

"Because *I* know what makes a woman beautiful," he drawled, joining them. His gaze dropped to her mouth for a moment, and her lips tingled in response. He only looked because of the new lipstick color.

Edwina shrugged. "Whatever you say." She nudged Mitch in the arm and motioned to her right. "Hal's here." She shot Lydia with a long, unnerving stare before heading off to tend to some customers.

* * * *

Mitch approached his friend, reached under the bar for a frosted mug, and poured the usual.

After shooting the bull a bit, Mitch kept an eye on Hal, knowing it was just a matter of time before he spotted Lydia. She looked great tonight—so great *he* couldn't stop staring at her. Faded jeans hugged her trim lower body. Her pale yellow tank top matched her silky blonde hair, which was tied back in a high ponytail. The tip of it swung and tickled her shoulder blades whenever she moved her head, which wasn't often right now. Her posture was as rigid as a fence post. With him, she could smile and be herself, but on her own…

He saw the exact moment when Hal noticed her. It reminded Mitch of the cartoon skunk Pepé Le Pew, whose eyes literally popped out of his head when he spotted the pretty feline whose fur was painted to make her look like a skunk.

Hal probably thought his attention subtle, but he couldn't be more obvious if he'd had an antenna on his head.

It wasn't long before Lydia noticed Hal's attention, and for a moment, Mitch thought she was going to turn away and dis him, but she didn't. As if suddenly remembering her "lesson" for the evening—to smile—her lips curved into the perfect greeting. It wasn't too blatant but more open than a courtesy smile.

If that didn't melt the frost on Hal's beer mug, then the man needed to have his eyes examined. Hal turned away first, his face bright red. Mr. Casanova blushing?

Lydia met Mitch's eyes and grinned, obviously pleased and proud of herself.

Mitch slapped the wet towel against the counter and scrubbed hard.

* * * *

Edwina picked up the phone. "Oh, hi, Lydia." She covered the mouthpiece with her hand and whispered to Mitch, "Maybe she called to cancel." She held up crossed fingers and squeezed her eyes shut as if in prayer.

He made a face and started a fresh pot of coffee. Edwina was still pissed at his suggestion that she take Lydia shopping for a dress to her reunion. Lydia had wanted *him* to go, as if he'd be caught dead browsing some chic Boise boutique or—God help him—the *mall*.

"Your sitter didn't show up?" Edwina said into the phone while looking at him, her brows lifted in surprise. "You have kids?"

Mitch knew he shouldn't eavesdrop and decided on the mature approach by moving just slightly down the counter under the lame pretense of organizing the bottles of hard liquor lined up against the mirrored shelves behind the bar.

"You take care of your dad?" Edwina asked. "Well, that explains a lot."

Mitch pretended to not pay attention.

"Oh, shoot. I was really looking forward to going shopping with you, too." She studied her red fingernails. "Yes, we'll definitely need to reschedule." She made a face for Mitch's benefit and stomped her feet like she was having a little tantrum.

Mitch shook a finger at her. "Be nice," he mouthed.

"Wait a sec," Edwina said suddenly. "I have a great idea. What about Gannon here?"

"What about me?" he asked, moving closer.

Ignoring him, she said into the phone, "He's off in about fifteen minutes. He can watch your dad." She gave him her sweetest smile that told him payback's a bitch.

He shook his head. Watching Robert St. Clair was *not* a good idea.

"Yes, he'd *love* to help you out. He's nodding his head yes even as we speak."

He glared at her.

"Yes, he is a sweetheart, isn't he? See you soon, Lydia."

She'd barely replaced the phone when he yelped, "Edwina, do you have any idea what you've just gotten me into?"

She twirled a long, dark strand of hair around her finger. "Pretty much, yeah."

"Her dad is about as agreeable as a hemorrhoid, I'll have you know."

"Then you'll be having just about as much fun as I'll be having, so we're even."

* * * *

"Are you sure this is okay with you?" Lydia pushed open the screen as Mitch and Edwina stepped onto the porch.

No, he wasn't sure. "No problem. I had nothing planned." Actually, he'd planned to spend the evening writing. He'd reached a crucial point on his work in progress and was anxious to get back to his computer.

She reached for his hand, rising on tiptoe to kiss his cheek. She smelled of vanilla and cinnamon, and he couldn't tell if she'd been baking or if it was her perfume. Without releasing his hand, she pulled him into the house. He caught Edwina's eye. Not liking what he saw there, he looked away.

Inside the foyer, Lydia said, "Dad's in the kitchen finishing his dinner. Mitch, I sure appreciate this." She gave him some relatively easy directions for taking care of Robert.

"Does he mind that I'm here?"

"Oh, no. In fact, he seemed pleased, which is a new one for him. Usually, whenever he learns someone new is coming to watch him, he kind of, well, has the senior-citizen equivalent of a tantrum. But he likes you, Mitch."

Edwina elbowed him in the side. He ignored it.

"Let me tell him good-bye. Then we can go."

When she disappeared around the corner, Edwina said, "She has the hots for you."

"We're just friends, Eddie. Don't get all bent out of shape over nothing."

"And don't you flatter yourself by thinking I give a shit."

"Uh-huh."

"Seriously, Gannon. She obviously hasn't been around the block very many times."

"Unlike you?"

She flipped him off. "I just hope she's not thinkin' she has a shot with you when *we* both know that she doesn't."

"I'm ready." Lydia stood in the doorway, purse in hand.

Mitch swallowed a guilty lump in his throat, hoping she hadn't heard the muttered conversation. From her smile, he figured she hadn't. He breathed out his relief.

* * * *

"Can I ask you a question?" Lydia asked, turning in the passenger seat to study Edwina's profile. The woman was perfect. Her exotic appearance probably drove men crazy—long, dark hair, creamy olive skin, almond-shaped eyes, voluptuous figure. Edwina was the kind of woman Lydia would have hated in high school because she'd have been so envious, the kind of woman who would have been mean to her in high school just because she was so gawky and shy.

Edwina glanced her way before returning her gaze to the road. "Go ahead, but whether I answer or not depends on the question."

"What did you mean on the phone? When I told you I take care of my dad you said, 'Well, that explains it,' or something like that."

The corner of Edwina's mouth twitched, and she stared straight ahead for several moments. Finally, she said, "You told me before that there's nothing going on between you and Mitch. Romantically, that is."

Lydia nodded. "That's right. There isn't."

The car turned onto Harrison Boulevard and headed downtown. "I'm glad to hear that, because—and don't take this wrong—but he'd never fall for someone like you."

Lydia blinked back sudden burning behind her eyelids. "Gee. Thanks."

Edwina glanced in her direction. "I told you not to take it wrong."

"How am I supposed to take it?"

Edwina sighed loudly. "Look. I'm just trying to give you some advice. You know, woman to woman. You seem like a real nice person, Lydia. If you say there's nothing going on between you and Gannon, then I guess I'll have to believe you. But..." The taller buildings of downtown Boise loomed up around the car. "On the teensy-tiny chance that you're full of shit and do actually have a thing for him, I gotta be straight with you. There's something about him you need to know."

Lydia clenched her hands in her lap, surprised Edwina knew the truth about Mitch.

"He tell you we used to date?" Edwina pulled the car into a parking garage.

Lydia blinked a few times until her eyes were accustomed to the dimness of the building's interior and until the shock of Edwina's words wore off. "You and Mitch dated?"

Edwina chuckled. "Nope. Guess he didn't tell you. Yeah, we worked together for almost a year before he couldn't stand it anymore and asked me out."

Lydia processed this information. She supposed it wasn't so unusual for a gay man to ask out a straight woman. It surely happened all the time in the guise of hiding their true lifestyle. Just this morning, on one of those silly talk shows her dad loved, a woman told the audience that her husband of thirty years was leaving her...for another man.

"H–How long did you date?"

Edwina shrugged, maneuvering the car through the narrow turnstiles and onto the third floor. "On and off for about a year. For a while there, I really thought he was the one." Her dreamy expression fled when she caught Lydia staring.

"What happened, if you don't mind me asking?"

"Of course I don't mind you asking since I was the one who brought it up. Oh, here we go." She slid the car into an available parking space and cut the engine. "I have a five-year-old son."

Lydia waited, expecting more. "And..." she prompted.

"Gannon doesn't date women with children."

I can't believe he dates women at all.

Edwina waved her hand back and forth. "Oh, he'd tell you I'm full of crap if you confronted him with that, but it's true. Every woman he's ever gone out with who has a kid never went beyond the second date. The only reason it lasted so long with us was because we worked together. Kinda hard to ignore the attraction in such close quarters, you know?"

So that was his story, eh? He didn't date women with kids, which left out most of the population. It was a good excuse, a good cover. "What does that have to do with me?"

"Your dad."

"Excuse me?"

"You're responsible for your dad just as I'm responsible for my Joshua, am I right?" At Lydia's nod, Edwina said, "If Mitch dated one of us, he might eventually have to take on those responsibilities, you know? All he wants to take care of is his pub and his parrot. He pretty much raised his gazillion younger brothers and sisters himself. Scared him off taking on more responsibility, you know?"

"That doesn't sound like the Mitch I know," Lydia said. In fact, the Mitch *she* knew was one of the most unselfish people she'd ever met.

Edwina gave her a sly look. "Yeah, well, I know him a bit better than you do, if you know what I mean."

Unfortunately, Lydia did know, and she didn't like the connotations. "If Mitch didn't like responsibility, he wouldn't have bought the pub," she said. "And you say he owns a parrot? Those birds live upwards of seventy-five years, I think. If he didn't want responsibility, he would have picked a hamster or something." Not that Mitch seemed like a hamster man.

Edwina's lips pressed tight over her teeth, and she waved her perfectly manicured hand. "All I know is that he and I were going along just fine until he met Joshua. Guess it hadn't occurred to him that if you date me, you date my son. One doesn't come without the other, you know?" She looked at Lydia, her expression hard. "You're in the same boat, Lydia dear."

"But Mitch and I—"

"Yeah, yeah. You're just friends. I know all that. I just wanted to be up front with you in case you put yourself into the position of getting your heart broken, too."

Lydia suddenly understood. "You're still in love with him, aren't you?" Sympathy seized her heart for this woman she barely knew. Edwina obviously needed to give herself a valid reason why Mitch had broken up with her. Not knowing the real story, she'd concocted one of her own.

Edwina smiled weakly. "Love is a strong word. Do I still want to jump his bones? Oh, yeah. I'd jump him in a heartbeat. I mean, what girl in her right mind wouldn't, you know?" She shrugged and pulled the keys from the ignition and dropped them into her purse. "I have to say, though, it drives me crazy when I see women panting after him at work. Gets me thinkin' real-mean thoughts."

The way Edwina looked at her, even though she had a smile on her face, shot something cold through Lydia's veins.

* * * *

His time with Robert St. Clair went much more smoothly than Mitch could have predicted. He'd expected Robert to be gruff, cantankerous, and demanding, when in fact he'd been anything but. Right now, the old man was being downright charming as he kicked Mitch's ass in checkers for about the tenth time in a row.

"No offense, sir," Mitch said after a particularly fast loss, "but I'm damn sick of checkers. In fact, if you lay one more king on me, I'm going to have to hurt you."

Robert chuckled and pushed the game board toward Mitch. "Sore loser."

"And proud of it." A flash of movement in the corner brought Mitch's attention toward the baseboards underneath the kitchen sink, but he saw nothing.

"How 'bout pushing this…chair to the windows and opening the…blinds for me?" Robert asked.

Glad to help, Mitch did what was requested, opening up the wooden blinds and letting the late afternoon sun stream into the kitchen. Outside, long shadows cut through the tall maple trees. Perennials in every shape, color, and size lined the perimeter of the yard. It all looked neglected and overgrown. Lydia obviously had no time to keep it up.

"Get me a beer, too, will you?" Robert commanded. "Grab one for yourself if you want."

Mitch's brows rose, but he did what the old man asked, thinking Lydia deserved sainthood for being at her dad's beck and call all these years. He pulled two cans from the back of the fridge. Sitting down opposite Robert, he popped the tops of both cans, sliding one across the table. Robert's worn fingers curled slowly around the can, and he lifted it to his mouth. Mitch kicked back in his chair and took a long swig, the cool liquid sliding down his throat.

After a few moments of companionable silence, or at least it would have been companionable had Robert not been studying him like a museum exhibit, Robert said, "Did you know Lydia wanted to be a lawyer when she was younger?"

Hmm. "No. I didn't know that." He frowned and tried to picture her making an argument in front of a jury but couldn't do it. Not that she didn't have the intelligence, she was simply too nice. He'd never met a nice lawyer before.

"She was interested in family law. Would have been good at it, too, with her keen mind. She's a smart...girl, my Lydia."

Mitch nodded his agreement. "Why didn't she pursue it?"

"She did. She was in her first year of law school at the University of Washington when I had my accident. She didn't think twice about dropping out...of school and coming home." He stared off into space, and Mitch could've sworn he saw the old man's lips quiver. "Didn't think twice," he said again.

"She's devoted to you, sir."

Robert nodded. "She's throwing her life away."

"I don't think she sees it that way."

"All she does is work and take care of me. She never dates. She never goes out with girlfriends. All she does is work and take care of me."

"She loves you."

He waved his hand. "She tell you about how all my

'babysitters'"—he practically spit out that word—"keep quitting?"

"She's, ah, shared with me her frustrations, yes."

"You know why they keep quitting?"

Mitch scratched behind his ear. "I have an idea."

"It's because of her."

Mitch sat back in his chair, startled, not expecting that answer. "What do you mean because of *her*? No disrespect here, sir, but I figured it was your doing."

"It *is* my doing."

Mitch pulled another long swig of the brew. The man was talking in circles. Maybe this was one of his bad days Lydia had warned him about.

Robert set his beer on the table. His unsteady hands weren't entirely successful, and the can toppled to its side with a quiet clatter. A thin stream of golden liquid spilled onto the table. Mitch grabbed a napkin mopped up the mess.

He waited for the old man to explain what he'd meant and continued to wait. He wondered if perhaps Robert was embarrassed for spilling his beer, or if he had simply forgotten the conversation. A movement in the corner flashed in his peripheral vision, but again he saw nothing when he turned to look.

Robert rapped his bony knuckles on the tabletop, getting Mitch's attention. The old man's gaze was shrewd and sharp, no sign of the slowness that sometimes affected him. "I need your word that this conversation...will not leave this room."

Mitch didn't like the sound of that, nor did he like its implication on the conversation to come. Clenching and unclenching his jaw, he nodded once, and Robert nodded back, satisfied with the unspoken assurance.

"I've been trying to convince Lydia...to put me into a home. You know, a retirement facility or whatever they call 'em these days. Used to be they were called nursing homes, but I suppose that term's...politically incorrect now." He took a long breath, as if summoning up the energy to continue.

He coughed a few times and waved Mitch off when he started to rise. "But she'll have nothing to do with that. Won't even…listen. Just turns around and leaves the room when I mention it. Never matter that she's wasting her life. She thinks it best for me to live here. Period. And when that girl makes a decision about something, that's it. I guess she was blessed, or cursed is probably the better word, with my stubborn head."

His chuckle was raspy. "Anyway, knowing I can't change her mind, I've been trying to force her hand. I figured if she couldn't get someone…to watch me while she is at work, she'd eventually get frustrated and be forced to put me in a home."

Understanding finally hit Mitch. "You've been scaring off the caregivers on purpose."

"Kind of slow on the uptake, eh, son?"

Mitch shrugged, taking it all in.

"I thought it was working, that she was finally beginning to see that moving me to a home would be easier on all accounts, but now she tells me that she's looking into working from home or quitting her job."

Mitch drummed his fingers on the table. "Why are you telling me all of this?"

"I want you to help me."

"Me? What can I do?"

"You can check out some local retirement facilities for me."

Mitch shook his head. "I don't want to go behind Lydia's back."

"You'd be doing her a favor, son. Think about it. I know about these 'lessons' you're supposedly giving her." He peered at Mitch through clear blue eyes beneath bushy white brows.

Mitch's brows rose, too, surprised Lydia had shared that information with her father. He cleared his throat. "Uh—"

Robert waved his hand in the air. "The girl clearly wants more out of life than…she's getting. But she can't have more with me around twenty-four hours a day." He gripped the rails of his wheelchair. "She didn't ask to have this burden. She doesn't...deserve to have this burden." He closed his eyes and took a deep, rattling breath. When he opened his eyes again, he stared at Mitch for a long time. "Please, Mitch. I don't want to spend the rest of my days, short as they may be, worrying about my daughter's happiness. Will you help me help her?"

Mitch peered out the window at Lydia's garden, seeing the flowers wilted and shrubs overgrown for lack of time. He reminded himself that she'd advertised for a gay date because she didn't think she had the time for a romantic relationship. He'd be doing Lydia a favor, he told himself.

Finally, he nodded. When Robert smiled, however, Mitch felt nothing but a knot of something unpleasant in the pit of his stomach, like he'd just made a pact with the devil.

Chapter 5

Mitch stepped onto the front porch as Lydia and Edwina pulled up to the curb. Realizing he'd been watching for them made Lydia hurry to grab her packages and exit the car.

"I hope that wasn't too long," she said, pushing the gate open with her hip and scurrying up the walk. "Was everything okay?" She tried to read his face and didn't like what she saw.

He sighed. "It was horrible, Lydia. He was a complete nightmare, ordering me around like I was his slave, swearing, throwing things..."

Her hand flew to her mouth, and she squeezed her eyes. When she opened them, she said, "Oh, Mitch. I'm sor—"

His full-blown belly laugh cut her off. "Oh, Lydia," he said between guffaws, "you kill me."

"Why is this funny? I thought he'd at least be nice for you, but—"

"Everything went just fine."

Her brows pulled together. "What?"

"It was great. He was great. Your dad and I got along fine."

"You were teasing me." She stepped toward him, her bags rustling at her sides, and kicked him none too gently in the shin.

"Ouch." He jumped back, still chuckling. Looking past her, he said, "Hey, Edwina."

"You survived," she said dryly.

"So did you," he added just as dryly. Lydia heard the undertones of sarcasm laced in the words. She'd suspected he'd talked Edwina into helping her out. Now she was sure of it.

"Where's my dad?" she asked.

His still-laughing eyes met hers. "He fell asleep in front of the TV during the news."

"I'm going to check on him. I'll be right back." She propped her various bags against the bottom step of the staircase and crossed the foyer toward the back of the house and the den where they kept the TV.

She found her dad just as Mitch had said. He snored softly, and his face looked at peace, unlike during his waking hours. Mitch had even thought to put an afghan across his shoulders. She smiled and tucked it closer around his still form. A man who didn't care for responsibility wouldn't have been so thoughtful.

When she came back to the foyer, Mitch and Edwina were engaged in a whispered conversation that stopped the minute she appeared in the hall. They'd done that earlier, too. Before, she'd thought nothing of it, but now, knowing their history...*Not your business.* Lydia pressed a smile into place.

"He's sound asleep. Thanks so much, Mitch. I mean it." She touched his sleeve, gently squeezing his arm.

"No problem. I was glad to help."

His gaze held hers. A pleasant humming buzzed in her ears as if to block out the rest of the world so that only she and Mitch existed. The spell was broken when Edwina slapped Mitch hard across the shoulder, the sound echoing off the high walls of the foyer.

"Ouch," he said, rubbing the place she'd hit. "What did you do that for?"

"Mosquito," she said.

He rotated his shoulder forward, and Lydia expected to see bug guts smeared across his white T-shirt, but there was nothing to be seen.

"I missed," Edwina said when Mitch glanced at her.

"Why'd you hit me so hard?"

"Big mosquito," she said.

Giving her an odd look, as if he didn't quite buy her explanation, Mitch turned back to Lydia and nodded at her assortment of bags.

"What did you guys do, buy the whole store?"

Lydia grinned and a blush warmed her cheeks. It had been so long since she'd shopped for anything but conservative business attire or lounge-around-the-house-type clothing. "You want to see what I bought?"

When she moved toward the stairs and her bags, Edwina stepped in front of her. "Oh, he isn't interested in all this girl stuff. Are you, Gannon?"

He shrugged. "Sure, I am."

Lydia tried to step around Edwina, but the woman stood firm.

"Clothes never look the same on hangers as they do on, so…keep that in mind when—" Edwina cleared her throat and glanced away.

Lydia whirled to face Mitch. "She's right. Would you mind horribly much if I tried them on for you? I'd really like a man's opinion."

"Them?"

"We couldn't decide on one dress, so I bought a few. I'll take back what I don't want tomorrow."

"Now, Lydia," Edwina said reproachfully, "remember how helpful—*not*—Gannon here was with the lipsticks."

"I know, but…" She smiled at him. "Would you mind?"

* * * *

Yeah, like Lydia really needed to beg him to see her do the *Pretty Woman* routine. "Not at all."

She gathered up the bags in her arms. "Edwina? Do you want to come upstairs with me?"

Edwina's face reddened, and she fidgeted with her hands. "No. I gotta go. Babysitter, you know." She strode across the foyer to the front door and was gone before either Mitch or Lydia could say good-bye.

Lydia frowned, staring at the closed door. "Is it just me, or was she acting really weird?"

Mitch took a moment before answering. "No, it's not just you." He wondered what her problem was. She'd had almost a guilty expression on her face, as if she'd been caught shoplifting or something. Hmm.

Lydia obviously didn't think anything more of it as she headed upstairs, the garment bags slapping against her thighs with every step. At the top, she turned and peered down on him.

"You're sure you don't mind?" At Mitch's wave of hand, she said, "I'll be right back."

He plopped down in the high-back chair against the side of the staircase to wait, which wasn't long. When he heard the unmistakable click of high heels coming down the stairs, he turned in his seat to look up.

Any expectations he'd had of seeing Lydia in goddess attire died when he glimpsed the pale-blue, ruffly thing she wore. The dress was about as conservative as a Glen Beck supporter and would have fit right in with the World War II generation.

He stood and met her at the bottom of the stairs. "That's, ah, a nice color. Matches your eyes." It was a stupid remark, but what else could he say, other than telling her it looked like something his grandma would have worn to church. She'd told him she had no sense of style, which is why she'd asked Edwina along. Apparently, she hadn't been exaggerating.

"You hate it, don't you?"

He couldn't lie. If Lydia showed up at her reunion in *that*, she'd never live it down. "Well, yeah."

To his surprise, she grinned. "I don't like it either, but it was Edwina's favorite."

"You're kidding."

She shook her head. "I told her what I was like in high school— you know, prude city?—and she thought it would be too obvious if I went back wearing something slinky or sexy, not that I'd feel comfortable in something slinky and sexy."

"Too obvious for what?" he asked.

She shrugged. "I don't know. Like I'm trying too hard or something, I guess."

He had no idea what that meant and figured it was a woman thing. "Let's see what else you have."

The next dress wasn't much of an improvement over the first. The third was even worse. By the fourth dress, Mitch realized the reason for Edwina's guilty look and sudden departure. A woman with impeccable taste when it came to clothes, Edwina for some reason had led Lydia to choose dresses from the senior citizen line. But why?

He was trying to figure out what his ex-girlfriend was up to when Lydia announced from the top of the stairs that this was the last dress.

Expecting another yawner, courtesy of Edwina's warped sense of God knows what, he was in no hurry to glance up. When he did, he was pretty sure his jaw fell open, and he struggled mightily to close it.

A vision in silver, Lydia descended the stairs, the shiny material whispering around her legs with every step. A strapless bodice pushed her breasts into gentle swells, and her pale skin glowed in the dim light of the chandelier overhead. A shimmery and voluminous skirt swept over her hips and legs, just sheer enough to see the shapely turn of knee and calf before stopping above her delicate ankles and strappy sandals. What held his gaze the longest, though, was her hair. Her glorious blonde hair flowed loose over her shoulders like strands of spun gold, each slight turn of her head causing the strands to catch the light and compete with the shimmers of the dress.

"My God," he croaked. "Cinderella." He wanted to yank her into his arms and kiss her senseless.

"This one's my favorite," she said in her sexy voice that nuzzled his hormones like hot tropical sand between his fingers. "It reminds me of something Grace Kelly would have worn." She floated the rest of the way down the stairs until she stood directly in front of him. "Of course, Princess Grace had nothing to prove. She was most certainly never a dork like I—"

He cut off her insecure ramblings by placing his finger over her pink lips. Just as he'd fantasized, her mouth was soft and warm. He slid his finger downward, gently tugging at her full lower lip.

Remembering his place and his recent promise to Robert and the unfortunate fact that he was supposed to be *gay*, damn it, he dropped his hand and stepped back. "Not a dork, Lydia," he whispered hoarsely. He barely recognized his own voice. "Beautiful. Classy."

Her wariness vanished, and she graced him with a bright smile. "You like it?"

"Uh, yeah. I like it." That was the understatement of the decade.

Lydia leaned forward and kissed his cheek, bringing with her the scent of vanilla and cinnamon. Her soft mouth was warm against his skin, and her breath fluttered his day-old whiskers. Just the slightest turn of his head would bring their lips together, he thought with an inward groan.

With that, she turned and fled up the stairs, and he half expected to see a glass slipper balancing on one of the steps in her wake. She paused at the upper landing and chirped, "Now all I need is Prince Charming."

As she disappeared in a whirl of silver and satin, Mitch seethed with jealousy over a man she hadn't even met yet, a man who might not even exist.

* * * *

Lydia stuffed the toilet brush back into its holder and used her elbow to flush while pulling off the yellow latex gloves one finger at a time. Gloves and bucket of cleaning supplies in hand, she headed for the utility room. Voices drifted inside from the front porch.

At the rare sound of her father's laughter, she figured Mitch must have stopped by. Her insides warmed as a glance to the street and the shiny black Harley confirmed her pleasant suspicions.

She paused at the screen door, peering through the grate to see him hunkered down on the top step, listening to her dad's softly spoken words.

"Well, I like this," she said, pushing the door open with her hip. The men immediately stopped talking. Mitch gave her a welcoming grin. "Here I am slaving away cleaning toilets while you two laze away the day on the porch. Must be nice."

Mitch stretched his arms overhead and stifled a yawn. "Yeah, life's rough, ain't it, Robert?"

Her dad made a sound that might have been a chuckle.

"How long have you been here, Mitch? I would've come out to say hello."

He unfolded his long legs and stood up. "And tear you away from the fun you were having? Not a chance."

She made a face at him. "Let me put this stuff away. Then I'll be back."

Reaching out, he took the empty bucket and mop from her, his fingers brushing against hers. His touch blipped her pulse into higher gear. "I can at least carry these."

"Gee. Thanks. Where were you about fifteen minutes ago when I was wrist deep in toilet water?"

"Conspicuously absent."

They laughed together. "Dad, we'll be right back." She wasn't surprised when he didn't respond. She brushed it off with a shrug.

"You're not working today?" she asked over her shoulder as Mitch followed her to the back of the house.

"Gave myself the day off. Too sunny outside to work."

Placing the cleaning supplies on a shelf in the utility room, she gave him a sly look from the corner of her eye. "Must be nice." She took the mop and bucket from him.

"Just one of the perks of being the boss."

"How long have you owned The Alley?"

"I bought it about three years ago thanks to working at Micron for ten years and selling off my stock at the right time."

She rinsed the bucket out in the sink and set it on the floor behind the door with the mop inside it. As they headed toward the front porch and her dad, she said, "Can you stay for lunch?"

He glanced toward the street, toward his bike.

"Oh," she said, trying to keep the disappointment from her voice. "You were heading off for a ride, weren't you?"

His brows rose at her guess. "Well, yeah. Actually I was. But now that you mention it, I am kind of hungry."

"You just like me for my food."

"Guilty as charged." He quickly dodged her left foot as she kicked at him, and hooked an arm around her waist, pulling her off her feet. "Will you cut it out?"

She shrieked as her legs swung out from under her, and their bodies slammed together at the hips. They were so close, his warm breath fanned her face. His gaze dropped to her mouth, and she moistened her lips with her tongue. He lowered her, and her body slid down his length.

Mitch's arm remained hooked around her waist. Lydia stared at her hands splayed across his chest. It rose and fell with his heavy breaths, his heart pounding beneath her palms.

Some inner force urged her forward, and their lips touched. His breath whispered against her mouth. Then he pushed away.

"Ah, Lydia." He cleared his throat.

Her face burned, and she slapped a hand over her mouth, backing away from him a few steps. "Oh, Mitch. I'm so sorry. I don't know what came over me, but—" She spun away, wishing the staircase would open up and swallow her whole. "God, I'm so embarrassed."

"Lydia, it's okay."

She shook her head, still too mortified to speak. Finally, she said, "I've never done something like that before. I mean, good grief, I can barely smile at a man at the pub, yet here I go…with you…Oh, God."

"Guess those manly man lessons I've been taking are paying off, eh?" He smiled, appearing none the worse for wear.

"You're not mad at me?"

"Just for the bruise on my shin."

Relief melted through her like warm sun on an ice-cream cone.

Before she could think of anything to say, he said, "Hold on a sec. I almost forgot the reason I stopped by." He practically sprinted out the door.

God. She was so pathetic. Sure, she'd been without male attention for almost longer than she could remember, but to confuse simple playfulness with attraction? Thank goodness Mitch was giving her those lessons—obviously, she had a long way to go.

* * * *

Mitch stood in the middle of the wide veranda and heaved a lungful of fresh air. *Damn.* He unclenched his fists and wriggled the tension out of his fingers.

That kiss…Wow. Who'd have thought such a chaste little peck could rock his world so thoroughly? If he hadn't pushed her away, he didn't know where that kiss might have led. Then his little ruse would have been over.

He blew out a long breath. He *wanted* this ruse to be over.

"Problems?"

Mitch swung around to find Robert St. Clair eyeing him over his bifocals. He'd forgotten the man was out here. "Ah, yeah." He sidled closer to the wheelchair and knelt. "Look, Robert, I know you asked me not to tell Lydia the truth about me," he murmured, glancing over his shoulder to make sure she was still inside, "but it's getting out of hand."

"You mean because she kissed you?"

Mitch blinked. He didn't bother asking how the old man knew about the kiss. Somehow, Robert St. Clair knew everything. "There's that."

"Did you kiss her back?"

Mitch just stared at him.

"Well, did you?"

He sighed. "No." But he'd wanted to. Historically, he wasn't a man who questioned his feelings. He felt something, he acted on it, but he hadn't with Lydia. He hadn't dared to. They'd built a fragile friendship. Kissing her wouldn't bring them closer. Kissing her would do quite the opposite, in fact.

"I need to tell her," he said.

Robert's hand clamped onto his wrist. "No!" he hissed. "She's just now starting to come out of her shell. If you tell her now, that shell will snap shut again. Just wait a couple more weeks. Until the reunion. She wants to go back a changed woman. I've seen the changes in her already, especially when she's around you." His grip tightened. "I don't think it would be good for her to find out the truth about you now, do you?"

"She'll hate me when she finds out."

Bony shoulders shrugged. "Probably. But better later than now, young man."

With a loud sigh, Mitch patted Robert's knee and stood, grabbing the bag he'd earlier set beside the porch railing. Inside the house, Lydia stood in the same place he'd left her, looking vulnerable and so damn innocent.

He held out the bag. She eyed it but didn't take it.

"Are we okay, you and me?" she asked, her voice quiet.

He grinned, wanting to set her at ease. "We're just fine, Lydia."

"Can we pretend it never happened?"

Yeah, he'd forget that kiss when hell froze over. "Pretend *what* never happened?"

Relief swept her expression, and she let out a long breath. Her smile shy, she took the bag from him. "What's this?"

"Open it."

She did and looked back up at him from under lifted brows.

"Mousetraps?"

"I know. You'd have preferred jewelry or chocolates, but..." He grinned. "The other night when I watched your dad, I saw a, ah, mouse in the kitchen." He waited for the squeal of fright. What was it about women and mice?

"And you want me to kill it? To smoosh its tiny little bones in these horrible contraptions?" She shoved the bag into his chest. "No, thank you."

"So you're just going to let it have the run of your house?"

She made a face. "No, silly. I'm going to trap it. I've done it before."

He raised his brows. "You're going to trap it." Lydia St. Clair was something else. He shouldn't be surprised that this woman with the patience of a saint when dealing with her crotchety father would be a rodent lover as well.

"Yes, and you're going to help me."

Chapter 6

Standing in the middle of the floor, Lydia planted her hands on her hips and looked around the room as if determining their next move. "Could you get the bucket and broom from the utility room?" She shook her finger at him. "And don't be getting any mean ideas about how you can use that broom."

He pressed a hand to his chest. "Lydia, you wound me." With a loud sigh, he did what she asked, and when he returned, she'd pushed Robert's wheelchair up to the kitchen table. Great. They had an audience for this absurd undertaking.

Lydia found the mouse almost immediately, and they spent the next half hour trying to trap it. Lydia would direct it with the broom, and he would upend the bucket on top of it. At least that was the plan. They were fast, but the mouse was faster.

"What the hell kind of rodent is that, turbo mouse?" Mitch asked, wiping his wrist across his brow, sweaty from chasing a stupid mouse. He needed to get back to the gym.

Robert sat, stony-faced, in his wheelchair as he watched their antics, but Mitch detected a slight grin on the old man's face.

Lydia squatted beside the kitchen door, looking more than a little frustrated. The mouse darted out in front of her, running across her shoe. Lydia squealed and leaped into Mitch's arms.

"I thought you said you weren't afraid of mice?" he accused with a laugh, disappointed when she pulled out of his arms.

"I'm afraid of anything that runs across my foot like that."

It was time to liven things up. Mitch stalked across the room in exaggerated tiptoe. "Crikey, mate," he drawled in an overstated

Aussie whisper. "I am the infamous mouse hunta, tracking a very dangerous species of rodent called"—he dropped his voice even further—"the kitchen mouse."

Lydia giggled as she followed him with the broom.

"We must be very, very cayaful. Oh!" He spotted the mouse behind the wastepaper basket under the desk. "There's the little rascal right thaya." With his free hand, he motioned for Lydia to step in front of him. "We must proceed with extreme caution, or else our little mousie will get away."

Lydia poked him in the shoulder with the broom handle as she neared their target. "Poor Steve Irwin would turn over in his grave if he heard that lame imitation of him," she whispered. Carefully, she pushed the broom across the floor toward the cowering mouse.

Mitch approached from the other side with the bucket.

"Careful. Don't let it get away," she whispered, "mate."

"I'm just the trapper, sweetheart," he said in his normal voice. "It's your job to make sure it doesn't get away."

"Oh, the poor thing is petrified. It's okay," she cooed at the furry little beast. "Isn't he cute?"

"It's a mouse, Lydia."

"That's such a man comment."

"I'll take that as a compliment."

"It wasn't meant as one." She pushed with the broom. "Now! Get it!"

He slammed the overturned bucket to the floor and held it there. He looked at Lydia. She looked at him. They burst out laughing. They slid to the floor, backs against the cabinets.

When he'd caught his breath, he asked, "Did we really just spend the last"—he glanced at his watch—"forty-two minutes chasing a mouse?"

She nodded, and they high-fived over the bucket. "Infamous mouse hunter, eh, mate?"

He leaned over and hooked her neck with the crook of his elbow and treated her to an old-fashioned noogie on the top of her head. When he released her, she hooked him with her arm and did the same to him. By the time they were done with each other, they were in hysterics again.

Robert watched them with an indiscernible expression on his worn face. Lydia noticed, too, and they pulled apart and straightened their hair, feeling like two kids caught necking behind the bleachers.

* * * *

Lydia hoped she didn't look as tired as she felt as she plopped down on a barstool at The Alley a few days later.

Mitch hailed her from the opposite end of the bar and headed her direction. "You look exhausted. You doing okay?"

When he reached for the bottle of her customary Chardonnay, she waved it away. "How about a coffee instead? I am exhausted, but thanks for noticing. My dad's been up to his old tricks again. Scaring away all the people I'm interviewing during the day and waking up all hours of the night. I swear, caring for the Tasmanian Devil would be easier than caring for that man."

Mitch didn't say anything, so she glanced up. A pulse ticked on the side of his jaw as he poured her coffee. "Mitch?"

"No luck finding someone to watch him, eh?"

She shook her head and accepted the heavy green mug from him, warming her hands on it even though the temperature outside was in the midnineties. "I just don't understand it. I know he can be a pain in the you-know-what, but his care level isn't all *that* extreme. You were able to look after him just fine. Now, granted, you didn't have to do anything like bathe or dress him, but still. He didn't give you any trouble." She sighed and sipped her coffee.

"Have you ever thought of putting him in a home?"

"No! I could never do that. Have you ever been to those places? They're cold and sterile, and they never have enough staff. I couldn't live with myself if I abandoned him like that." She was a bit hurt he could even suggest it.

His hand covered hers. "I'm just worried about you, okay?" His touch was warm and comforting.

She sighed. "I'm sorry. I'm just tired."

He squeezed her hand and released it. "Who's watching your dad right now?"

"One of my neighbors. She must have felt sorry for me when she saw me hauling the garbage out this morning, looking like I'd just been run over by a freight train. She has a free afternoon and offered to keep Dad company for a few hours. So, here I am."

"You have the whole afternoon in front of you, and you chose to come see me? I'm flattered."

"I love hanging out with you." She flashed him a wide smile.

"The feeling's mutual, gorgeous." He tapped the counter in front of her and left to attend to some other customers.

He'd called her gorgeous. She looked like crap. She'd seen herself in the mirror this morning and declared herself a disaster area. She wore no makeup, and her hair hung flat and lifeless around her shoulders.

Gorgeous. Right. The man needed to have his eyes examined.

Still, his words made her insides go soft.

She glanced around the bar, looking for Edwina, but didn't see her. She caught a man looking at her from a table across the room. She recognized him as Mitch's friend, Hal, if she remembered correctly. He had a laptop computer set up at his table, and his hands had paused on the keypad. She was about to look away, as was her customary habit, but she forced herself to smile.

Feeling rather pleased with herself for that little interaction, she thought for sure Hal would approach her after that and prepared herself for the conversation, but he didn't. In fact, when she peeked his direction while pretending to get something from her purse a few minutes later, he was gone.

"Did your friend leave?" she asked Mitch when he came over.

Mitch looked out over the sparse dining room. "Guess so."

"What did I do wrong?"

He shrugged. "I have no idea. I've never seen him do that before."

"I must have done something wrong." Her shoulders slouched. She couldn't attract a man if she wore skintight leather and carried a whip.

"Lydia, look at me." She did. Anger mottled his face. "It's not you. Trust me. You did perfect. You look fantastic."

Her lips tugged into a smile. "You are such a liar, Mitch Gannon. From now on remind me not to believe a word you say."

His expression mimicked Hal's, and he stalked away to help a customer on the opposite end of the bar. Curiously dejected, Lydia stared after him a while, but he didn't turn back her way.

Ordering herself not to read anything into the gesture, she sipped her coffee and focused on keeping her posture relaxed and friendly like Mitch suggested.

Someone tapped her shoulder, and she turned with a smile, assuming it was him. But it was a man she'd never seen before.

"May I?" he asked, motioning to the empty barstool beside her.

Her face heated up, and she nodded stiltedly, unable to speak.

"Can I buy you a drink?" he asked.

"No." *Ouch.* That came out much harsher than intended. The man's brows lifted, and his expression changed from friendly to cautious.

She tried to remember what Mitch had been teaching her and said, "I mean, I'm just having coffee, but you're, um, welcome to join me."

The man's expression relaxed into an easy smile again. "I'm Neil," he said, holding out his hand.

She hesitated only briefly before taking it. "Lydia."

"I've seen you in here before."

Her blush deepened. "I, um, know the bartender. The, um, owner. We're friends." God, she sounded as intelligent as the coffee mug she held in her rigid hands.

Neil was an attractive man with blond hair and a healthy tan, like he did a lot of work outside in the sun. His blue eyes watched her as if waiting to hear more, but she couldn't think of anything remotely interesting to say. Small talk had never been her forte.

Thank God Mitch arrived to save her. "What can I get you?" he asked Neil.

"A Henry's on tap and a refill of the lady's coffee."

As Mitch poured steaming coffee into the mug, he said to both of them, "So how about this warm spell we're having, eh? I don't know about you, but I wouldn't mind a day or two of rain."

Neil shook his head and held up two fingers in the sign of a cross. "Don't say that, man. I own a landscaping business and don't work when it rains."

There was her in, Lydia thought, silently thanking Mitch for providing her with conversation tips so she didn't come across as a *total* dork. "What type of landscaping do you do, Neil?"

"Primarily residential, but I have a couple of commercial clients. What do *you* do when you're not here?"

"I'm a paralegal," she said.

"And what exactly does a paralegal do in her spare time?"

"I don't really have a lot of free time these days. My dad is ill, so I'm taking care of him."

Neil nodded his understanding. "He's staying with you until he gets better?" His compassionate expression said he thought she was nice for doing this.

Lydia smiled. "No, I've been caring for him for about five years now. It's pretty much a full-time job."

Mitch set Neil's beer in front of him, his eyes narrowing as Neil downed it in one quick gulp. He slapped some bills onto the table and stood. "Well, it was nice meeting you, Lydia." He tapped his watch. "I forgot I have an appointment. Gotta run." He nodded to Mitch. "Thanks for the beer, man. Catch ya later."

* * * *

The expression on Lydia's face as that jerk walked out on her just about tore Mitch in two. With clenched fists, he silently swore if that guy ever so much as walked past the bar again, he'd pop him.

Lydia's bottom lip trembled, her gaze blank. "See?" she said. "I scared him off."

"He was a jerk."

"He seemed nice."

"He seemed like a jerk. If he was nice, he wouldn't have left after hearing about your dad."

Lydia's eyes widened. "That's why he left?"

He shrugged. "That's my guess."

She ran the tip of her finger around the rim of her coffee mug. "Why am I even bothering with all this? I mean, what guy will be able to accept the responsibility I have?"

"The *right* guy."

Her quivering hand told him she doubted that guy existed. It *would* be difficult. As a whole, men were jerks. They were immature, selfish, and irresponsible. And that was just the nice ones.

She looked so dejected, and he couldn't blame her after the way Hal had left and after that asshole's hasty exit. A small part of him he didn't want to acknowledge was glad, though. It made absolutely zero sense, but he hated the thought of another guy coming on to her and being interested in her. Even though that was why she was here and why he was helping her, he still didn't like it.

He wanted to bring a smile back to her pretty face. "When do you have to get back home?"

She glanced at her watch. "Not for another hour or so. Why? I don't think I'm up to another lesson today, Mitch. I really don't. In fact, I'm thinking this whole thing is—"

"We're going on a field trip today."

Her blonde brows lifted, blue eyes doubtful. "What? Where?"

He grinned and said, "Give me ten minutes to finish off my shift. Then we're out of here."

Fifteen minutes later they headed out onto the street and the bright afternoon. Sunlight reflected off the sidewalk, forcing him to pull the sunglasses from the crown of his head. Lydia did the same.

"Where are we going?" she asked as they walked to the nearby parking garage.

"You'll see." They headed up a couple of flights of stairs. "There," he said, pointing.

She followed the direction of his finger. He saw the tentative smile on her mouth. "You're giving me a ride on your motorcycle?"

"That's the plan. You game?"

"I've never ridden on one before."

"But you want to, don't you?" He nudged her in the arm.

"Well, I suppose you could talk me into it." She nudged him back.

"Do you mind if we run over to my place real quick so I can change? I always smell like beer after work."

She dipped her head and peered at him from beneath her lashes. "Now *that's* a line if I ever heard one. Can I trust you alone at your place?"

Thankfully, he hadn't taken off his sunglasses, because his eyes would've given away his surprise at her words. She'd never in a million years say that if she knew he was straight. Like he'd told her dad, this had gotten out of hand.

He forced a grin. "Never trust a man alone at his place, babe."

She nodded. "I'll remember that. Wait, speaking of babes…" She reached up and pulled the rubber band from her ponytail, then bent forward from the waist and ran her fingers furiously through her long mane of silver-gold hair. She straightened, her hair flying up in an arc before settling onto her shoulders. She looked like she'd just crawled out of bed after wild sex.

Again, he was glad she couldn't see his eyes.

"I wanted to look like a true biker babe. Oh, wait." One at a time, she rolled up the sleeves of her T-shirt, revealing her slim shoulders. "There. Now, I'm ready, Mr. Harley Man."

He wondered if she had any idea how sexy she looked. He doubted it. She wasn't one to strut her stuff. Releasing the kickstand, he climbed onto the bike and started it up. He directed Lydia on behind him. He swallowed hard as her long leg swung over the seat. Her thighs tightened briefly against the black leather before relaxing with her knees pointed outward. In a gravelly voice, he explained where to place her feet and filled her in on some of the rules of motorcycling.

As he backed out of the parking space, he focused on every single place her body touched his—her inner thighs grazing his hips, her long fingers grasping the sides of his waist, the heat of her skin penetrating the material of his shirt, her soft breath tickling his neck.

This would be sweet torture. What had he been thinking? He shifted on the seat, another problem arising.

Damn. His body hadn't gotten the memo that he was supposed to be gay.

* * * *

The big bike accelerated with a rush of power Lydia had only heard about with these motorcycles. To keep from flying backward, she slid her hands around Mitch's torso. His abdominal muscles tensed. Was it because of her touch?

Maybe it made him uncomfortable to be touched so intimately. But if he'd once dated Edwina…Hmm. It didn't make sense that Mitch would date women to hide the fact he was gay. She knew him well enough by now to know he was an honest and up-front man and wouldn't do anything that wasn't on the up-and-up.

Maybe Edwina was the victim of wishful thinking, and she and Mitch hadn't actually "dated." Heaven knows, Lydia had been a similar victim ever since meeting him.

You can't make a leopard change its spots, she'd told herself over and over after she'd kissed him. If it were possible for a gay man to go straight, however, someone like Edwina would be the catalyst, not a plain Jane like her.

The wind whistled in her face, blowing her hair and whipping it every which way but demure. She would need some righteous detangler when she got home.

As the motorcycle picked up speed, the bike's energy surged beneath her and between her legs, the vibrations pervading her body, and she had the silly thought that this was the closest she'd had to sex in a long, long time. The idea was so preposterous she laughed, the sound soaring into the wind.

Too soon, Mitch slowed the bike and turned into a neighborhood of modern homes with fantastic views of the city and valley. Pulling into the driveway of one of the smaller but more beautiful houses on the block, he cut the engine, and she climbed off the bike, unable to stop smiling.

He swiveled on the seat, saw her grin, and chuckled. "Enjoy yourself?"

She nodded. "That was awesome!"

He swung his leg over the bike and climbed off. "Almost better than sex, ain't it?"

Lydia blushed. Had he read her mind? "I'll take your word for it."

His grin faded, and she saw herself reflected in the lenses of his dark sunglasses. Even in miniature, she looked pathetic. She was glad she couldn't see or hear the inner workings of his mind.

He downed the kickstand with the toe of his scuffed black boot and headed toward the house, keys dangling from his hand.

She followed him to the front door. "This is a gorgeous house, Mitch." Although it wasn't at all her style with its modern lines and feel, it looked exactly like the type of place she'd pictured Mitch living in. It was simple and uncomplicated, just as he liked it.

As he pushed the key into the lock, she asked, "Will Jacque be here?"

He shot her a funny look. "Well, yeah. He's always here."

She tried to hide her surprise. "Oh. I guess I figured you lived alone."

He held the door open for her, and he followed her into a black-tiled entryway. "His bedside manner isn't that great, but he's decent company."

Thinking of Jacque's bedside manner—great or not—was almost as bad as thinking of Mitch having dated Edwina. Both were images she'd just as soon stayed pushed into the far recesses of her imagination.

Her body cooled in an instant as the air-conditioning swept over her. Drawn shades kept the interior dark, and it took a moment for her eyes to adjust from the brightness outside.

"Ignore the mess," he said as tile gave way to hardwood floors and they stepped into a simply furnished living room of black leather, glass, and chrome.

She supposed his house was a mess by her standards, but then again, she spent much of her waking hours inside her house, so it was either stare at the mess or clean it. Mitch, on the other hand, had a life. He had better things to do with his time than clean.

She predicted her house would always be clean.

Hastily straightening up some newspapers and grabbing up a few carelessly tossed items of clothing from the living room, Mitch said, "I keep telling myself to hire a maid, but I haven't taken my own advice yet."

"What's the saying, 'Creative minds live in messy houses,' or something like that?"

"Well, from the looks of the place, I'm damn creative, aren't I?"

Lydia peered around the modern home. She neither saw nor heard any sign of Jacque. While a silly little part of her was jealous, her curiosity was stronger. "Where's Jacque?"

Mitch thumbed his finger over his shoulder. "When did I tell you about him? He's not usually a topic of regular conversation unless someone stops by here."

Odd comment, she mused and peered past him. "You mentioned him the first time we met at Alive After Five. You said something about him waiting for you at home." Still not seeing Jacque, she stepped around Mitch, but all she saw was a giant birdcage and a computer workstation set up in what used to be a dining room.

Distracted for the moment from her desire to meet Jacque, she asked, "Is that where you do all your writing?"

When Mitch didn't answer, she turned around to find him staring at her with a stricken expression on his face. "Mitch? What's wrong? You look sick."

He closed his eyes and muttered something under his breath. Opening them again, he said, "I can't do this anymore. Lydia, meet Jacque." He moved around her and headed toward the birdcage. "Jacque is my parrot."

Chapter 7

"Jacque is your parrot? But I thought you told me—" Lydia looked back and forth between the colorful bird and Mitch. This misunderstanding didn't account for his dark expression.

"I'm not gay, Lydia."

She blinked. "What?"

He sat on the edge of the paper-strewn desk. "I'm not gay."

Lydia's feet rooted in the middle of the room. "When you say 'not gay,' do you mean you like women, too—I mean, I know you and Edwina used to date and—"

"I'm straight."

If a person's color could truly drain from her body, then Lydia figured hers pooled on the floor at her feet. She wrapped her arms across her chest, and she stepped backward. Heat buzzed her face as if she'd just downed a shot of hard liquor.

"How straight?"

"One hundred percent."

Her hand crept up to her throat. Her pulse thumped against her fingertips. "You really aren't gay? This isn't some sort of weird Mitch joke?"

He shook his head. "I'm sorry I misled you."

Her heart skipped a beat as she remembered. *"My last lover's name was Eddie, and my longtime companion, Jacque, is waiting for me at home."* Eddie was Edwina. Jacque was a parrot.

"You lied to me." She took another step backward, farther away from him.

Her stomach churned as if Martha Stewart was in there with an electric mixer. All those fantasies she'd had about him being straight, which had been so harmless at the time, now hung like a noose around her neck.

"I never really lied. I—" He hung his head. "I'm sorry."

Looking him in the eye was too humiliating, so she dropped her gaze to his broad chest, which was humiliating in an altogether different way. Finally, she settled for staring at the floor between them.

Betrayal stung her eyes. "Why did you pretend to be gay?"

"It was all just a misunderstanding at first, the result of a practical joke—"

Her head snapped up, and she glared at him. "A joke? And *I* was the butt of that joke, am I right?" Bad memories from her childhood crashed into her mind. She wrapped trembling arms around herself and dug her fingers into her biceps, the anger bruising her skin.

"Lydia, this joke had nothing to do with you. It—"

She shook her head with such force her sunglasses flew from her hair and landed with a clatter on the hardwood floor. She didn't bother to retrieve them. "I need to go now."

"I understand how upset you must be, but—"

"No. You can't *possibly* understand how upset I am. You can't possibly understand what it was like to be the butt of countless jokes and pranks as a kid. I thought you were above them, Mitch." Her voice caught on his name.

"It's not like that at all. Please let me explain what happened."

She held up her hands. "I don't care. I don't want to hear anything you have to say, okay? I just need to go. Now."

She grabbed her purse from the couch and walked to the front door, using every bit of mental discipline she possessed to refrain from sprinting.

"Lydia," he said as her fingers curled around the doorknob, "let me give you a ride."

She didn't turn around. She didn't want to see his handsome face.

She didn't want to see his beautiful mouth—the mouth she had once kissed…

"No!" The thought of sitting behind him—a straight man—on that big, sexy motorcycle was enough to make the Virgin Mary blush.

* * * *

Lydia said nothing to him the entire ride, nor did she look at him. She stared out the passenger window, her body turned as far away from him as possible. She'd agreed to the ride only because he'd reminded her of the three-mile walk and the ninety-degree heat.

He couldn't blame her for being so upset. It was just as he'd known it would be when she found out the truth.

No, it was worse.

He'd expected to see the hurt and feelings of betrayal in her eyes, but he hadn't expected to see so much pain. Her blue eyes had widened with shock and horror when the truth had finally sunk in.

He was relieved to have everything out in the open but saddened at what this meant to their friendship, or what was left of it, if anything.

He swung the convertible into a loading zone near his pub. Leaving the engine running, he said, "Lydia," but that's as far as he got before she leaped out of his car and slammed the door behind her, not once looking back.

Again, reality and his expectations collided. He'd expected to feel saddened by her reaction and ultimate rejection of him once she found out he was straight.

He hadn't expected this aching hole in his gut, nor the almost unbearable pain in his heart.

* * * *

She felt so stupid. All the signs had been there, clear as the lenses on her glasses—no one other than her "knew" he was gay, she'd never caught him looking at another man but had caught him looking at her. He'd dated Edwina, and he never talked about other men. Nothing about him had suggested he was gay. She thumped her head a few times on the steamy bathroom mirror, her damp hair wiping off some of the fog. "Stupid, stupid, stupid," she muttered. How could she have been so blind? How could she have been so trusting?

Her terry-cloth robe loosely tied around her waist, she sat down on the toilet lid and pressed her face into her hands, her long, wet hair sliding forward to whisper against her knees. After Mitch dropped her off, the first thing she'd done was jump in the shower, hoping to cleanse away the shame and humiliation, but it hadn't worked at all. If anything, she felt worse. The more she thought about all the times she'd fantasized about him, all the times she'd wished she could be the woman to "change" him, and all the other stupid things she'd done and said, the more she wanted to crawl into a mousehole and disappear.

He'd only met with her because of a joke. Her skin crawled as it had so often during her adolescent years when she'd been the butt of cruel jokes or pranks. How many times had she come home crying and locked herself in this very bathroom until her tears ran dry?

Here she was again.

"Lydia." Her dad's raspy voice echoed in the small, steamy room through the intercom on the wall.

Sighing, she pressed the talk button. "I just got out of the shower, Dad. What do you need?"

"Mitch is on the phone."

She closed her eyes, angry at the traitorous butterflies in her stomach that leapt and pranced at the mere mention of his name.

"Tell him I'm not home."

The intercom clicked with static, but her dad didn't answer. Good, she thought with a nod of her head. That was that.

That *wasn't* that, she realized a few minutes later when the intercom buzzed again as she stood naked in the middle of the bathroom.

"Mitch will be over in about twenty minutes," her dad's voice said into the speaker, and the intercom clicked off again.

She froze and felt naked in an altogether different way. For a moment she could do nothing but stare at her shocked expression in the mirror. Twenty minutes. Twenty minutes. Could she get dressed and out of the house in twenty minutes? No, she couldn't leave her dad. What to do? She couldn't possibly face Mitch yet. She didn't want to ever face him again.

She tugged a wide-toothed comb through her hair, yanking it through the snarls and bringing tears to her eyes. She didn't want to see him. For whatever reason, he'd played a joke on her and lied to her. She'd trusted him, and he'd lied to her. She couldn't decide if anger, hurt, or humiliation was at the forefront of her feelings. It was pretty much a toss-up.

By the time she finished combing her hair out, anger had moved to the head of the pack. She dressed in record time, not bothering to put on makeup. What was the point?

She'd gone halfway down the stairs when a knock came at the front door. She stomped across the foyer and opened the door. She didn't meet Mitch's eyes as she commanded in a firmer voice than she felt, "Go away." She shut the door in his face before he could say a word.

He knocked again.

"I don't want to see you, Mitch. Go away!"

"Lydia, please. I have to talk to you."

She closed her eyes and rested her forehead on the cool panels of the door. "Sorry. Not home." Her voice shook, along with her entire body. Directing herself to remain strong, she pulled down the shades on both sides of the door to make her point.

"You don't think you're…being a bit childish?"

Lydia whirled around at the raspy voice. Her dad had wheeled his chair into the foyer. "I don't care if I am," she snapped. "He lied to me."

"Maybe he had a good reason."

"What could possibly be a good reason?"

Her dad shrugged his bony shoulders. "Guess you'll never know, will you?" He wheeled himself into the den.

Lydia peeked through the curtains to see Mitch heading down the porch stairs and onto the sidewalk.

"Good riddance," she huffed with a conviction she didn't really feel. She watched him climb onto his Harley, looking more masculine and sexy than a man had a right to look. How could she have ever possibly believed he was gay?

Mitch turned his bike around on the sidewalk, and for a moment it was pointed directly toward the house. One rev of his engine would bring the big machine straight up the walk and onto the porch. She held her breath. He stared her way for a moment, and then he reached up and pulled his sunglasses down over his eyes. The rumbling of the Harley's engine permeated the walls of the house as it sped off down the street.

She flung her damp hair behind her shoulders. So what? Like she'd told him quite clearly, and with only the slightest tremble to her voice, she didn't want to see him.

So why were her insides such a royal mess?

* * * *

On Saturday, feeling cooped up and with too much on her mind to stay inside, Lydia headed out to the garden, a place in which she'd spent far too little time during recent months. Weeds, overgrown perennials, and out-of-control vegetable plants competed with each other, the weeds appearing to have the upper hand.

Hands on hips, she studied the landscape, trying to decide where to start. Right where she stood was as good a place as any, and she dropped to her knees and yanked the nearest offending weed.

She'd planted vegetables last May with good intentions, but good intentions didn't replace a good thinning and liberal dose of fertilizer. The rows of lettuce were going to seed, as had the broccoli. The zucchini didn't seem affected by her lack of attention, however, and multitudes of the cylindrical squash hung on the overgrown vines.

Basket in hand, Lydia began thinning out the growing ranks of zucchini, mentally reminding herself to make a giant batch of bread and give the rest of the vegetables to her neighbors.

She flicked an earwig off one of the larger squash. Crushing it with the toe of her gardening clog, she muttered, "Disgusting creature."

"I hope you weren't referring to me," came Mitch's deep, familiar voice from behind her.

Straightening, she pulled her shoulders back and prepared herself to see him again, but didn't immediately turn around. Her treasonous heartbeat picked up a few notches.

Finally, when she was relatively sure she could face him without hurling the basket of zucchini at his head, she turned. "If the shoe fits…" Her words trailed off suggestively, and she set the basket down because it was too tempting.

He wasn't looking at her face, but her legs, his gaze slowly traveling upward from her shoes. The once-over unnerved her, turning her legs to jelly.

Unwilling to let him see that he fazed her in any way, shape, or form, she shrugged and reached for the weed bucket. "You should call before dropping by. I could have saved you a trip." She shot him a fake smile.

"Actually, I came by to see your dad." His brown eyes looked darker than normal.

"What? Why?" Her fingers tightened over the handle of the bucket to keep them from shaking.

"He called me. Asked me to stop by."

"Why?"

Mitch shrugged, the movement tightening his white T-shirt across his shoulders. "You'll have to ask him that."

"Well, I can't. He's inside taking a nap. So I guess you'll just have to leave."

He plopped himself onto the wooden swing perched in the shade of the apple tree. "I'm in no hurry."

"Suit yourself. Just don't expect me to entertain you." She stepped over a crowded row of carrots and radishes.

"Lydia, we need to talk."

"Why? Will talking make you feel better?"

"Well, yeah, it probably will, but—"

"Then I'm not interested."

His quiet chuckle surprised her. "You're one stubborn woman."

She whirled around so sharply that her ponytail slapped her in the face and stung her eyes. "What I am is mad." She pointed her trowel at him. "You lied to me. I thought you were my friend."

"I am your friend," he said, his face partially hidden in the shade of an overhanging tree branch.

"Friends don't lie to their friends, Mitch."

"I know that, and I'm really sorry."

She gave a very unladylike snort and knelt to pull weeds. Her garden was just full of pests today—tall, handsome ones notwithstanding.

"If I talk, will you listen?"

"You can talk." She jerked an especially stubborn weed from its roots, causing her to fall backward and land on her bottom in the dirt.

She glanced sideways at Mitch through the edge of her sunglasses to see his reaction to her graceful move. He stood up from the swing and moved toward her. If he planned to help her up, he could save his manners for someone who appreciated them. She maneuvered back to her knees and resumed weeding.

Mitch squatted down in the row next to hers. She was about to tell him she didn't need his help but then decided if he wanted to get down and dirty with the weeds and other pests, she certainly wouldn't stop him. He'd probably feel right at home.

For a moment she watched his strong hands work in the dirt, admiring the way his forearm muscles rippled and tensed with every movement.

"I didn't know it was a gay ad when I answered it," he said.

"How could you not know? It was in the Men Seeking Men section. I hardly think you'd not have noticed it unless you're completely blind and daft." She tipped her sunglasses and raked her gaze slowly over him, letting him deduce what he liked from her look.

"Hal asked me to answer it."

"Your friend at the pub? He was in on it, too?" Her stomach lurched at the thought.

"No. He just…started the whole thing."

"I'm listening."

"He was mad at me for setting him up on a really bad blind date not long ago and wanted revenge. So he pretended to be writing an article for the paper—he's a journalist, if you didn't know. Said he was working on a story about dating in the age of the Internet. I thought it was a lame idea, but…Anyway, he asked me to help him out as a favor since I owed him one."

He didn't speak for a few moments. "I didn't know it was a gay ad, Lydia. That was part of the joke."

She blinked a few times, watching a spider crawl across a broad rhubarb leaf. "After you realized I thought you were, um, gay, why didn't you tell me then that you weren't?"

He sat back in the dirt, an elbow resting on the worn knees of his jeans. "I don't know. You caught me off guard, for one. Don't you remember me spitting out my latte?"

Her mouth twitched. "I do remember that."

"Since I figured I'd never see you again, I thought I'd let you off gently, and that would be that."

"But you asked me out for drinks. Why?"

He shrugged. "I guess I just…liked you, Lydia. Felt bad for you, like I'd let you down."

"So you felt sorry for me. That's why you agreed to help me out and pretended to be my friend."

"I *am* your friend, whether you believe it or not. And I didn't feel sorry for you. I…empathized with you."

She sat back on her heels and studied him from under the wide brim of her straw hat. "Explain."

"I told you how I grew up with six younger brothers and sisters. Well, guess who was pretty much responsible for raising them?" He directed a thumb toward his chest.

"Your parents weren't around?"

"They were, but they were so busy working multiple jobs to make ends meet, they didn't have much time for the kids. That all fell on me."

"You sound resentful."

"Do I?" He looked surprised. "Well, I was, certainly. I can't tell you how happy I was once my youngest brother was old enough to take care of himself. I left home so fast you can probably still see the skid marks on the street outside the house." He lifted his head and peered at her. "When you told me about your dad and how you spent so much time taking care of him that you didn't have time for yourself, well, I understood exactly how you felt, because I'd been there myself."

She turned her face away and grasped a weed at its roots and pulled. Then she pulled another and another. She didn't want to *not* be mad at him anymore. If she wasn't mad at him, then what would she be? She certainly couldn't be his friend anymore, not after the fool she'd made of herself getting all gooey in front of him.

"We've known each other for three weeks now," she said. "Why didn't you tell me the truth earlier?"

He was silent for so long she thought he might not answer. She tilted her head and looked at him. He watched her, his dark eyes squinting in the bright sunshine.

"I was afraid to."

She snorted.

"I thought you'd hate me, Lydia."

She harrumphed under her breath.

"*Do* you hate me?" His words were hesitant.

For a time, the only sound was a persistent robin on the fence surrounding the yard and the sound of her trowel striking the dirt between the rows of vegetables. No, she didn't hate him. She wanted to hate him, but…

Deciding it was safer not to answer his question, she waved the trowel in the air between them. "You've explained yourself, apologized, and I appreciate it. Your conscience is clear."

"It's far from clear. Do you hate me?"

Her fingers gripped the trowel, and she stared at the weeds before her. "I don't know how I feel about you, Mitch. I'm hurt, and I'm mad, but…no, I don't hate you."

Relief flooded his eyes. He gave her a small nod and resumed his weeding. They spent the next hour working in adjacent rows without speaking a word to each other. It wasn't an altogether uncomfortable silence, but Lydia found herself more than aware of his body just several feet away.

He didn't have gloves, nor a hat or sunglasses, yet he worked just as hard as she did, if not harder, finishing his row and starting on another before she'd finished hers. Of course, if she hadn't spent so much time staring at him from beneath her hat, she might have been able to keep pace.

Finally, she heard her father stirring through the portable monitor she carried on her belt. She stood, wiping the dirt from her legs and making a point of not looking at Mitch just in case he was looking at her legs again. She wanted to be mad at him. If she wasn't mad, she would have to deal with her confused feelings toward him, feelings she didn't understand or need.

"My father's awake," she said, brushing the dirt off her knees and shorts. "Since you came to see him, you can keep an eye on him while I go grocery shopping." She shot him a phony smile as she pulled off her gardening gloves.

"Are we okay, you and me?" he asked, his gaze boring into hers, so intense she had to look away.

Nothing was okay, least of all her heart. She picked up the basket of zucchini. "I need to wash these," she said, heading toward the house.

* * * *

Ten minutes later, Mitch watched Lydia's car back out of the driveway. "Why do we *park* in driveways and *drive* on parkways?" he asked, turning to face Robert St. Clair, whose wheelchair faced the kitchen window overlooking the backyard and Lydia's gardens.

Robert stared at him with a blank look on his face.

Mitch shrugged. "I'm a writer. I wonder about these things."

"Maybe you should…quit worrying about the peculiarities of the English language and figure out how to right matters between you and my daughter."

"I'm working on it."

"Well, work harder."

Mitch shot him a dry look. "It's not that simple. Things aren't the same between us anymore."

"They probably won't ever be the same," came the scratchy reply.

That wasn't a comforting thought.

"Did you…make those calls we talked about?"

Mitch dropped into a chair at the table. "I made a few."

"Well?"

Mitch scratched behind his ear. "Sir, I have to tell you, this whole thing makes me pretty uncomfortable. I'd rather you get Lydia to do that for you."

"She won't."

"Maybe, but I can't lie to her about anything else. I'm already on her shit list."

Robert's tired blue eyes peered out the window, and Mitch wondered if the old man was looking at something outside or watching memories from within. "When my daughter was younger, while the other kids were out drinking and dating, she was babysitting to earn extra money. She loves kids. Always talked about having several." He turned and pierced Mitch with a clear stare. "Does that scare you, young man?"

"Why would it scare me? It has nothing to do with me."

"Lydia tells me you don't date women with children."

"That's a bunch of BS." He scratched his neck, very itchy all of a sudden.

"Is it now?"

Mitch shifted in his chair.

"My daughter's dreams have changed over the years. She never discusses her career or starting a family anymore. Now all she wants is to go to that damn reunion. That's as far as she's looking into the future, Mitch. Which is why I need to get out of her hair."

"I doubt she sees you as a burden."

Frail shoulders shrugged. "I'm sure she doesn't. But eventually she will."

Chapter 8

"Lydia needs your help right away!" came the gravelly voice over the phone the next evening as Mitch finished his shift at The Alley.

Mitch's hands gripped the receiver. "Robert? What's wrong?"

"Hurry!" The connection clicked off.

Wiping his hands on the rag he had slung over his shoulder, he waved Edwina over. "I need you to cover for me. Call Ben. Ask him to come in early."

"What's wrong?"

"Lydia needs me."

Edwina's eyes narrowed into slits as he sprinted off.

A few minutes later, he and the Harley screamed across town toward the St. Clair residence. His mind raced along with his bike's engine, conjuring up all sorts of horrid imaginings. Was Lydia okay? Had she been hurt? Had they called 911? Fear gripped his heart, and his belly was tight with worst-case scenarios.

What seemed like hours later, he screeched to a halt in front of the old Victorian. After jamming the kickstand down, he sprinted up the walkway and onto the veranda. Not bothering to knock, he yanked open the front door and barreled through.

"Lydia! Robert!" he yelled, pausing in the foyer to look around and see if everything appeared normal. It did, but that didn't slow his racing heart.

Within moments, footsteps pounded from above, and Lydia ran down the stairs. "Mitch? What's wrong? What's going on?" She didn't stop moving until she was right in front of him.

He gripped her arms and studied her from head to toe. "I came right away. Are you all right?"

Her blue eyes squinted at him. "Of course I'm all right. Are *you* all right? You look like you've seen a ghost." She rested her hand on his arm. "You're even shaking."

"I am?" *I am?* He blinked to clear his head. "Your dad called and told me to get over here right away. That you needed my help."

She frowned. "What?"

"Yeah, he said—"

Lydia took off toward the den. "Dad?" she called out. Mitch followed at a quick jog.

Robert St. Clair glanced up from the book laid open on his lap, looking perfectly healthy and well. "What's all the racket? Good grief, I can't even hear myself…think."

Mitch and Lydia paused in the doorway, shoulder to shoulder, both breathing heavily with worry.

"Dad? Did you call Mitch and tell him to get over here?"

One bony shoulder shrugged. "I don't know if those were the exact words I used, but yes. I did ask him to stop by."

"So nothing's wrong?" Mitch asked, his heart rate returning slowly to its normal, steady state. "You told me Lydia needed my help right away." He tried to keep his voice from sounding accusatory, but was unsuccessful.

Robert seemed unperturbed. "She does need your help."

Lydia scrunched up her nose. "I do? With what?" she snapped.

"With the zucchini bread."

"What!" Lydia and Mitch barked in unison.

Robert flipped a page of his book. Lydia tapped her foot, waiting for Robert's response. "You were complaining about all the zucchini we have and how long it would take you to turn it all into bread. I thought you could use some help." He didn't look up but continued his ruse of reading.

"Dad, that's ridiculous. I don't need help, and I wasn't complaining."

Mitch shook his head. "You mean I rushed all the way over here to *bake?*" His voice rose to a level he hadn't used since his disciplinarian days with his siblings. "I dropped *everything* I was doing and even left my shift *early* to get over here fast enough. Robert, I mean no disrespect, but this is–is—" He fumbled for a word that wasn't too offensive.

A gentle hand on his arm broke his unsuccessful chain of thought. Lydia peered up at him. "You dropped everything because you thought I needed you?" she asked softly.

"I thought you were hurt. Dying even. Of course I dropped everything."

She lifted her hand and trailed her fingers across his jaw, her touch causing his breath to catch in his throat. "That's really sweet."

He blinked, and then he understood, sending a silent thanks to the old man across the room without breaking Lydia's gaze. He wondered what she'd do if he pulled her into his arms and kissed her so long and so deep that they'd have to come up for air. He wondered what it would be like to kiss her long and deep. He wondered...

As if reading his thoughts and suddenly remembering she was supposed to be mad at him, she broke all contact and jerked away, moving toward her father.

Mitch couldn't help grinning. She could act as pissed off as she wanted to, but that definitely wasn't anger he'd seen in her eyes just now.

"Dad, that was a rotten trick to pull on Mitch, and I want you to promise never to do it again."

Robert nodded submissively. "Yes, dear. I'm sorry, dear." As Lydia straightened the blanket across his legs, Robert caught Mitch's eye over her head, his lips twitching into a wrinkled grin.

Mitch shook his head in amazement. Robert might be old, and he might be ornery, but he was one smart SOB.

* * * *

Something cold and wet splatted on the back of her neck. She'd pulled her hair up into a loose bun to keep it out of her way as she mixed up a megabatch of zucchini bread.

She lifted her hand and touched her neck, hoping Mitch had flicked her with a wet towel, but she felt something soft and squishy against her fingers. Pulling her hand down in front of her face confirmed her suspicions. He'd thrown a glob of grated zucchini at her.

Turning, she watched him feed cut zucchini into the food processor like nothing was amiss, his back to her.

"You can tease all you want, Mitch, but I'm not biting. I'm still mad at you. The only reason I asked you to stay is because I felt bad about what Dad did to you."

When he didn't respond, she turned back to her bowl and cracked two eggs into the mixture. Another glob of zucchini hit her, this time in the back of her head.

She whirled around, but again, he pretended to be intent on his own work. She pulled the goo from her hair and tossed it into the nearby garbage can.

"That was only moderately funny the first time. You're losing steam. Now cut it out." There. She'd sounded firm and annoyed enough that he'd stop this nonsense.

Splat. Cold, gooey vegetable hit her in the back of the neck, this time sliding down under the collar of her sleeveless blouse. Lydia pressed her lips together. Fine. Two could play this game. Scooping up a handful of dough from the mixing bowl, she crossed the kitchen and tapped him on the shoulder. He spun around and held up his hands, as if expecting retaliation.

Deliberately, she scraped the rest of the zucchini out of her hair and off her neck and held it out to him, palm up. "The zucchini is supposed to go *in* the bowl," she said.

He peered into her eyes a moment then dropped his head to look at her hand. It was enough. She pulled the doughy mess from behind her back and slapped it on top of his head, smearing it into his scalp. He roared in surprise, and she leapt back. He touched his hair, pulled back his hand and saw the sticky mess between his fingers.

She couldn't help the laughter that burst from her lips when she saw his amazed expression. "You asked for that, Zucchini Man. Or should I say 'Boy' because, I swear, you're worse than a child, Mitch Gannon."

With slow, methodical movements, Mitch reached behind himself and scooped up a huge mound of grated zucchini.

She shook her finger at him, backing up as she did. "No, no, no. We're even now."

A diabolical grin lit up his face. "Not yet we're not."

"Mitch, that's enough," she said, trying to sound tough, which was hard as her lips tugged upward at the corners. "What? You can dish it out, but you can't take it?"

"Oh, I can take it all right. But I'd prefer to dish it out."

She shrieked as he lunged for her, circling the table until it stood between them. She sprung to her left, and he did the same. She ricocheted right. So did he.

They played this cat-and-mouse routine for several laughing minutes, until Mitch finally said, "Lydia, your hand is bleeding."

Startled, she lifted her hand and glanced down at it, dropping her guard momentarily, but it was long enough for Mitch to bound over the table like a wild animal and grab her by the wrist.

"Sucker!" he hissed, laughing at her shock and surprise.

"You lying piece of...of..." She couldn't think of an appropriate description for him. Besides, she was laughing too hard to think straight.

She tried to pull away, taking baby steps and pulling him along with her until he'd backed her against the refrigerator. "You wouldn't dare," she said, eyeing the glob of goo he held between them, out of breath from the game.

"Wouldn't I?" He closed the gap between them, still holding her wrist.

"It's a waste of perfectly good zucchini," she said, watching as his eyes roved over her, obviously trying to decide where the mushed veggie would best go.

"There's plenty more where that came from. Who's going to miss it?" His eyes stopped at her chest, and he grinned like the Cheshire Cat—wicked, devious, and charming at the same time.

She looked down at her lemon-yellow blouse then back up at him. His brown eyes crinkled at the corners. She pressed her free hand to her chest, holding the material of her blouse against her skin.

"Don't *even* think about it," she commanded in her sternest tone of voice, one that would have most men quaking in their boots.

Mitch Gannon, however, wasn't like most men.

* * * *

Lydia's chest rose and fell with her heavy breathing, and Mitch couldn't keep his gaze from dropping to the shadowy area beneath the open top button of her blouse.

"Mitch," she said, her voice breathless and sexy as all get-out, "you're hurting my wrist." A pained expression replaced the twinkle in her eyes.

Silently cursing himself for breaking the spell of their fun, he let go and stepped away.

"Who's the sucker now?" she whooped as she grabbed his hand holding the zucchini goo and shoved it at him, splattering wet vegetable all over his neck and shirt.

Her triumphant smirk fled the minute he snared both her wrists with one hand and pressed her against the refrigerator, pinning her hands above her head. His knee thrust between her thighs, giving her no room to maneuver.

Her eyes sparkled with laughter and apprehension over his next move.

"Now, dearest Lydia. Just how am I supposed to react to that?"

She giggled. "You can call it even. You started it."

"Yes. And I'll end it."

"That's not fair."

"Life's not fair."

Getting an idea, he grinned and reached behind her. She squirmed away, unsure what he was up to. When the sound of the ice maker in the door came on, her blue eyes widened.

"Mitch. *Not* a good idea."

He brought his hand between their bodies, holding a palmful of crushed ice in front of her face.

"I say we call a truce," she said, her gaze not leaving the ice.

"And I say you're in no position to be calling anything."

He held the ice above her face, letting cold water drip onto her nose. She turned her head sideways to avoid the drops. He poised his hand above her heaving chest.

"Don't you dare," she whispered, trying to look mad, but her eyes betrayed her.

He just raised an eyebrow and dropped the ice into her shirt above the top button. Lydia shrieked and tried to wriggle free as he rubbed the ice into her skin. As her body moved beneath his, his pulse quickened from more than the roughhousing. He became all too aware of his hips slanted against hers and his knee planted between her thighs. He was also extremely aware of his hand. He had been smearing the ice into her torso and his fingers now rested in the valley between her breasts.

He realized she no longer struggled to get away. She stared up at him, her heavy breathing expanding her chest against the fabric of her damp blouse and against his hand. Her heart hammered beneath his fingers.

Keeping his hand still, he slowly lowered his head. Her eyes closed as their lips touched. Her mouth was warm and soft, just like he'd known it would be.

It was a chaste little kiss, but it left him wanting more. Knowing he treaded on dangerous territory here, he lifted his head.

Her eyes opened slowly, as if drugged.

"I've been wanting to do that for a very long time," he told her, his voice surprisingly husky.

"You have?"

"Yeah, but it's kinda hard to make a move on a woman when you're supposed to be gay."

One corner of her mouth turned up. His eyes fell to her lips again, and they parted under his gaze.

"I'd really like to kiss you again." This was a new thing for him, being with a woman who had so little experience. He wasn't used to asking permission. Normally, he just went for it if he knew the woman was receptive.

Lydia's neck arched, and her lips parted farther in silent acquiescence. Tilting his head slightly, he pressed his mouth to hers, this time tasting her with his tongue. She tasted faintly of cinnamon, as if she'd been chewing gum or sucking on a cinnamon candy.

Moving slowly, his fingers splayed wide, grazing the tips of her nipples. They pebbled at his touch, and she gasped against his mouth.

His jeans tightened almost painfully at the crotch, and he rubbed against her as if that would quell his growing hunger, but it just made it worse when she moaned at the contact between her legs. He let go of her wrists and slid his free hand behind her, cupping her bottom and pulling her closer. Her arms wrapped around his neck, and she made little mewing sounds against his mouth as his thigh ground between her legs. Wanting, needing to feel more of her, he released the top button of her blouse and slipped his hand inside and under her simple cotton bra. Her soft, warm breast fit perfectly in his palm.

She stiffened beneath him and turned her head to the side, breaking the kiss.

"Am I going too fast?" he asked softly.

Her nod was barely discernible. She avoided his eyes, and he felt like a teenage boy who'd pushed his new girlfriend's boundaries just a bit too far.

He released her and stepped back to give her some space. "I'm sorry."

She shook her head. "Don't be." Her voice was breathy and sexier than ever. After a moment, she said, "Since I've known you, I thought you were gay. Even though there were times I wished you weren't—like the time I kissed you"—she blushed and dipped her head—"I'm not used to thinking of you as straight. I'm used to just being your friend. This is really weird for me."

His gut gave a jolt. "So we're friends again? You're not mad at me anymore?"

A tiny smile tugged on her mouth. "I wouldn't have kissed you if we weren't friends again."

"Friends don't generally kiss each other on the mouth, Lydia."

A blush swept up her face, and she sat down at the kitchen table. Her yellow blouse gaped open, revealing a white, lacy bra. Her chest rose and fell with her ragged breaths, expanding the slight swells of her breasts. He clenched and unclenched his hands and forced himself to look away.

"What does that make us then?" she finally asked as she buttoned her shirt. "More than friends?"

Being "more than friends" meant dating. Dating Lydia could never be a casual thing. It was an all-or-nothing thing, and that scared him to death. "I don't know" was his safest answer.

Her slight smile disappeared.

"But it might be worth exploring," he said.

The smile returned. "Remember I don't have much experience in this area, Mitch. I mean, I never dated in high school, not once. In college, I had a boyfriend for a while, but…And I've told you what my social life has been like since moving back to Boise." She drew a big zero in the air with her index finger.

"It's nothing to be afraid of." Or so he told himself. "Why don't we just continue on with the friend thing, and if we happen to kiss now and then, well..." He raised and lowered his eyebrows a couple of times, then chuckled. "We'll just see what happens. How's that?"

* * * *

Studying in her firm's library, Lydia reread the paragraph about some obscure law for the umpteenth time, unable to focus. Her cell phone vibrated in her jacket pocket. Retrieving it, she eyed the number calling and smiled.

"Hi, Mitch," she greeted the reason for her unfocused state. They hadn't spoken since their zucchini fight and that amazing kiss on Saturday. She'd begun to worry she'd scared him off somehow.

"Hey, gorgeous. What are your plans this evening?"

"Oh, gosh, I'd have to check my social calendar because it's so full, but..." She giggled. "Why? What do you have in mind?"

"I thought we could take my bike up to the mountains."

She pictured herself on the back of his motorcycle, her body pressed against his, and a slow tingle spread upward from her toes. "Oh, that sounds really nice, but I can't get anyone to watch Dad at such short notice."

"Your neighbor can't help?"

"I don't even want to ask her. She's done so much for me lately."

Silence reached across the line. "How about dinner at your place? I could stop by the fish market and bring over some salmon steaks. I grill a mean salmon."

She smiled, picturing him in a chef's hat and apron and nothing else. Shocked at her train of thought, she said, "Oh, shoot. I just remembered. Dad has massage therapy at six. He's usually pretty out of it afterward. Can I take a rain check?"

"If I didn't know better, I'd think you were avoiding me. Does this have anything to do with our kiss the other night?"

Surprised he'd connect the two unrelated issues, she said, "No, of course not. I'd love to see you, Mitch, but my dad…Well, my life kind of revolves around him and his schedule."

"Speaking of your dad…he told me there's a new retirement community going up near—"

"I am not dumping my dad in one of those places, Mitch. I've already told you that."

"But have you ever looked—?"

"I don't *need* to look. I'd be abandoning him, and I won't do that. I'll never do that. I promised my mother when she died that I'd take care of Dad." She chewed on her bottom lip. "I won't put him in a home."

Mitch was quiet for a time. Then he said, "I'm working the evening shift the rest of the week. If you can, why don't you head down here? I'll buy you a drink."

She was still rather perturbed that he'd even brought up the dreaded *R* word. "I can't promise anything," she said.

"Just tell me you'll try. I want to see you."

* * * *

A few nights later, Lydia stopped by The Alley after work. Nabbing one of the few available stools, she realized how much more comfortable she was here than she used to be. She wouldn't call herself a social butterfly yet, but she was making progress thanks to Mitch.

Thinking of whom, she scanned the area behind the U-shaped bar for him. He stood at the opposite end and hadn't yet seen her. Edwina, on the other hand, had noticed her. Instead of smiling or waving a greeting, she just nodded her head slightly.

All of a sudden, everything clicked. Edwina was jealous of her, *had* been jealous of her. Lydia just hadn't paid much attention because she'd "known" Mitch was gay. Edwina's green-eyed monster hadn't really been an issue. But now...

Her gaze sought out Mitch as he rearranged and organized the liquor shelves. He still hadn't seen her.

He was such a good-looking man. Could he truly, possibly be interested in dating her when he could have Edwina with the snap of his fingers? It was hard to imagine.

She'd have to ask him sometime why he and Edwina had broken up. Edwina had told her it was because he didn't date women with children, but Lydia didn't really buy that. Mitch wasn't that shallow. If he was, why would he want to date *her*? Her dad was just as much a responsibility as a child, perhaps more so.

Edwina passed her with a tray of empty glasses. "Hey, Lydia. Haven't seen you in here in a while."

"It's hard for me to get away sometimes."

"Your dad?"

Lydia nodded, and Edwina smiled, seeming to relax a bit.

"Guess what?" Edwina asked, moving one of the glasses on her tray that had slid precariously close to the edge. "Mitch and I are going out on Saturday."

Lydia's stomach dropped about a foot. "What? You–you mean like a date?"

"Yep," Edwina drawled, transferring the tray to her other hand. "We're going to the Hawks game. Do you like baseball, Lydia?"

"I'm not really a fan."

With a little shrug, Edwina said, "Mitch is a *huge* fan. He told me once he could never date a woman who didn't understand the game. *I* love baseball." With that, she flounced away, her hips swaying provocatively as if to tell Lydia she could never compete in the sexiness department, which was probably true.

A yucky feeling in the pit of her tummy, Lydia pondered the idea of Mitch going out with Edwina, when the reason for her yucky feeling noticed her and came down the bar.

"Well, hey," Mitch greeted. "You look fantastic."

She couldn't help smiling at the compliment. "Thanks."

"How long have you been sitting here?"

"Not long."

Was he still attracted to Edwina? No. He wouldn't have kissed *her* if he was interested in another woman. Then again, he'd told her when they began their lessons that dating didn't mean committing yourself to one person. Dating was just a way to get to know someone.

"I'm glad you could get away," he said, wiping his hands on a rag.

She shrugged. "Dad doesn't seem to mind the current caregiver too much, or maybe it's the other way around. Either way, she agreed to stay a bit late tonight." She cleared her throat. "Edwina tells me you two are going out on a date on Saturday."

Even in the dim light, she could see his neck redden. "Uh, she told you that?"

She nodded, waiting for his answer and trying to untie the jealous knot in her heart.

"It's not really a date."

"She said it was."

"We're just going to a ball game together. She won free tickets on a radio program."

Lydia supposed that should make her feel a little better. This whole dating scene was so confusing.

Mitch pulled a wineglass from the rack overhead. His blue button-down shirt stretched tight across his shoulders as he moved. She'd dug her fingers into those shoulders when he'd kissed her. She let out a long breath, remembering. They'd shared a kiss, which to her was a mind-blowing thing. Apparently, Mitch felt different. Maybe with men, a kiss was just a kiss.

She sighed again. Life had been easier as a social hermit.

Pushing all confusing thoughts to the back of her mind, she made a decision. If Mitch wasn't going to place any great significance on that kiss, then neither would she. She straightened on her stool. "So, what's my lesson tonight, teacher?"

His brows drew together. "Lesson?"

She nodded. "My reunion is less than two weeks away. I'm starting to worry I won't find an escort."

"But…" He cleared his throat. "Why don't you just go alone? You don't really still need a guy to take you, do you?"

"Mitch. I already told you I could never go there alone," she said in hushed tones, seeing Edwina hovering nearby. "My mom convinced me to go to my prom alone, saying that modern girls did that all the time. But that wasn't true. I was the *only one* there without a date. I got teased unmercifully. If I go to the reunion alone, they'll all think I'm the same pathetic girl I was back then."

"You're not pathetic, Lydia. And why do you care what those people think? They mean nothing to you."

"I know it's stupid, but it does matter. I've often wondered what it would have been like to be somewhat popular in high school. I was *so* the complete opposite of popular. I don't think I could face those people by myself. Uh-uh." She shook her head. "No way."

He said nothing but rubbed down the counter in front of her, which already looked perfectly clean and polished to her eyes.

"I wish you didn't have plans that weekend." Her voice trailed upward at the end in a sort of wistful question.

He looked up and met her gaze. "I could never bag out on my friends, Lydia. None of us has missed that ride in the nine years we've been doing it."

She sighed, disappointed but not surprised, and wishing she had friends like that—friends who would go out of their way to be with her. Oh well. Her few close childhood friends had all moved away. She'd left her college friends behind in Seattle. Since returning to Boise, she hadn't had the time to develop any close friendships with anyone until now, with Mitch.

"But for what it's worth," he went on, "I would have loved to be your date."

She smiled at him. She'd love that, too. Oh, boy, would she love that. "So, what's my lesson tonight?"

"You don't need any more lessons, Lydia," he said, his voice clipped.

"Of course I do. I need all the help I can get."

"All you have to do is be yourself."

"I've been doing that for years."

"Have you?"

She stared at him. "What's gotten into you? You act like you're mad at me."

"I'm not mad at you. I just—Never mind." He cleared his throat. "Like I said, you don't need any more lessons. You just need more practice."

"Practice?"

He nodded. "When a guy approaches you, just be yourself, and see what happens."

"What if no one approaches me?"

"They will. Trust me on this."

"And you know this how? I've come in here half a dozen times, and only two men have ever come over."

His gaze swept over her from the tip of her head to her waist— below that was hidden from him by the counter. Even so, that look made the area between her legs tingle in response.

"Because you've let your hair down," he said.

She reached up and touched her hair. "You serious? Men are that shallow?"

He laughed, his dark eyes crinkling at the corners. "The sooner you realize that, dearest Lydia, the better. Seriously, though, it's not just that you're wearing your hair down – it looks terrific like that, by the way."

She blushed.

"It's also your attitude. You just seem more relaxed and approachable."

She had to admit some of the men at work had seemed more attentive to her today, even though she'd worn the same conservative navy suit she'd worn countless times before. Maybe it was the silk fuchsia blouse she'd paired with it.

She held up a finger. "Men." She held up another finger. "Shallow. I'll remember that."

Mitch grinned and left to attend to other customers.

"Is this seat taken?" a deep male voice asked on her right.

The voice sounded remotely familiar, and when she turned toward it, she saw why. It was Mitch's friend Hal.

Lydia's body burned from the inside out, and a flush crept up her neck. "No. I mean, go ahead. Take it." Stop babbling and shut up, she commanded herself.

Hal sat down on the stool and motioned to her nearly empty wineglass. "Buy you another?"

She shook her head, and his expression grew guarded. "I don't like to have more than one if I'm driving home," she explained, and his face relaxed again.

"Beautiful and sensible. I like that in a woman." His grin was infectious, and she couldn't help smiling back. He said she was beautiful.

"Hal King," he said, holding out his hand. His grip was firm.

"I'm Lydia St. Clair."

He released her hand and rested an elbow on the bar. "Nice to meet you, Lydia St. Clair. You know, I've been meaning to introduce myself to you for quite a while now."

"You have?"

He nodded. "It took me a while to get up the nerve."

"You're kidding. Why?"

Shrugging, he said, "Most of the times you're in here, you don't seem all that interested in anything other than Gannon over there. Thought for a while that you and he might be…" His blond eyebrows lifted suggestively. "But then I heard that he and Eddie are getting back together, so I figured I'd come over and introduce myself."

Mitch and Edwina? "Mitch told you that?" she asked, hoping she didn't sound too love struck. Her gaze sought him out where he was mixing up drinks while talking and laughing with a couple of customers on the opposite side of the bar.

"Eddie did. Just tonight, in fact. I always figured they'd get back together someday. They always made such a great couple."

She cleared her throat. "Well. Yes. I had heard they'd dated before." *Stop babbling.*

"You know, I'm just going to risk it," he said.

"Risk what?"

"Asking you to dinner this weekend."

She blinked. He watched her, his grin wavering slightly when she didn't respond.

"You mean a date?"

"We don't have to call it a date, if you're not comfortable with that term. Just two people having dinner together to get to know each other better."

That definition must be something men learned in Dating 101. Hal's cell phone rang before she could respond to his invitation.

"Damn," he said. "Would you mind? I've been waiting for this call all day."

At her nod, he held up a finger. "Hold that thought," he said and swiveled on his stool to answer the phone in some semblance of privacy.

Mitch set a frosty mug of beer in front of Hal, who was too enrapt in his quiet conversation to notice.

"Want another glass?" He motioned to her wine.

She shook her head. "I'll take a coffee if it's fresh."

"Honey, for you I'll make a brand new pot." He grinned. "So, what's up with this?" He cocked his head toward Hal.

"You won't believe this, but he asked me out to dinner."

His smile faltered slightly. "Really? Why wouldn't I believe that?"

"I don't know. Maybe it's that *I* can't believe it. I mean, it's been a long, long time since I was asked out on a date." She kept her voice quiet so Hal couldn't hear, not that he paid any attention. Mitch had told her he was a journalist. From the way he furiously scribbled on a narrow notepad in his hand and the serious look on his face, he was probably doing an interview of sorts right now.

"Well?" Mitch asked.

"Well, what?"

"Did you say yes?"

"I didn't have the chance to say anything before his phone rang."

"And he took the call?"

"He said it was important."

He rolled his eyes. "Right. So, are you going to?"

"Am I going to what?"

He blew an exasperated breath. "Are you going to say yes to going out with him?"

"Oh. I don't know. What do you think I should do? I mean, you know him. Is he a nice guy?"

"He's...a ladies' man, Lydia."

"That's bad?"

"It depends what you're looking for. He'd probably be a fun date. He's a good conversationalist. He likes to have good time. But if you're looking for long-term..."

Lydia stared at him in disbelief. "Listen to you. You're the one who's been telling me to stop thinking long-term and just go with the moment, have fun."

He shrugged and filled the coffee carafe with water. "It's your call. Go out with him if you want."

The part of her that hoped he'd act jealous was disappointed. "Does he"—she tipped her head Hal's direction—"does he know that I'm the one who placed that ad?"

Mitch shook his head. "He has no clue."

The cell phone in Hal's hand snapped shut, and he turned back to her. "Sorry 'bout that. I've been trying to get a hold of that guy for a story I'm working on." He nodded at Mitch. "Hey, Gannon. Thanks for the beer."

"How are things?"

"Busy. Hey, do you mind making yourself scarce for a while? Lydia and I here have something private to discuss." His thick brows lifted almost imperceptibly.

Mitch caught her eye before leaving her alone with Hal, or as alone as they could be in a semicrowded bar.

Hal turned to face her, his blue eyes bright with the unspoken question.

The thought of going on a real date with a man she barely knew caused her toes to curl up in her sensible shoes. What would Mitch advise her to do?

She didn't have to ponder that long because she knew the answer. "What time this weekend?" she asked, feeling coy and sophisticated.

Chapter 9

Mitch caught himself staring at the wall behind his computer rather than the monitor and realized his fingers were unmoving on the keypad. He wondered how long it had been since he'd typed a word.

He stretched his fingers and did a couple of shoulder rolls to loosen the kinks in his neck. He'd gotten up early this morning to write, but he hadn't gotten anything done. At least, he hadn't written anything worth reading.

Scrolling up a few pages and skimming the words that were supposed to flow into coherent sentences and interesting paragraphs, he saw it was nothing but garbage.

Usually when he wrote, even when he wrote badly, his mind was completely focused on the task at hand. The phone could ring in the other room, and he wouldn't hear it. Someone could knock on his door, and it wouldn't register.

This morning, however, was different.

His mind wasn't on his writing. It was on Lydia.

This coming Saturday night she was going on a date with Hal King, Mr. Casanova himself. *And* she had the nerve to be excited about it. While *he'd* be at the Hawks game with his friend, Eddie, *she'd* be on a *date* with Hal.

He'd tried to act supportive and happy for her, because getting her dating again had been the point of all the "lessons." At least that had been the point in the beginning. But Lydia and Hal?

She should be going out with *him*.

That thought hit him from out of nowhere, and he straightened in his ergonomically correct computer chair, one he'd spent a ridiculous sum of money on in the hopes of protecting his back and neck from the rigors of being a many-hour-a-day writer. He circled his head a few times and felt all the kinks. Maybe the chair had been a waste of money.

Lydia was never far from his mind anymore. *She should be going out with me.* Hmm. He was attracted to her, yes. Most definitely yes. Stopping their kiss the other day had been pure torture.

Did he want a relationship with her? Did he want a relationship with any woman right now? Every romantic relationship he'd ever been in had made him feel tied down, burdened. It was like dragging around a twenty-pound weight—doable, but not the most comfortable feeling in the world.

He knew that didn't say good things about his character. He was thirty-two years old, and the thought of being in a long-term, committed relationship scared the crap out of him.

His life was great the way it was. He was his own boss, chose his hours. He set aside time every day, rain or shine, for his passion—writing. When he wanted to take his Harley out for an afternoon, he did it. There was no one to stop him. He spent his money how he wanted, and he liked it that way.

Before he could edit his actions, he'd grabbed his cell phone and speed-dialed her number. She answered on the third ring.

"Hello?" Her husky voice sounded sleepy, like he'd just woken her up.

Shit. Mitch glanced at the digital time readout at the bottom of his computer screen. 6:22 a.m.

"Hey, Lydia. It's me. I didn't realize how early it was."

"Mitch? Is something wrong?" She sounded more awake now, but her words were still drawn out and tired.

He had the sudden image of waking up to her each morning and hearing her sleepy "good morning" in his ear with that sexy, husky voice of hers as they snuggled together under warm covers.

Blinking that image from his mind, he said, "No. Nothing's wrong except that I've woken you up. Sorry about that. I've been up for a while and—"

"You're writing?"

"Trying to."

At the end of a yawn she said, "You're so disciplined. You'll be published before you know it."

He chuckled, liking her positive attitude. "Yeah, well, tell that to the editors in New York."

He heard a rustle of something that was probably sheets and blankets and pictured her cuddled in her warm bed, her arm wrapped around a feather pillow, her eyes closed as she held the phone to her ear.

"So, what prompted you to call me at this ungodly hour? Don't you realize we women desperately need our beauty sleep?"

"Some women, maybe," he murmured, liking the thought of her half asleep in bed. Did she sleep in a nightie or maybe just a T-shirt or nothing at all. That thought had more than just his heart rate rising.

He recalled her question. "I wanted to know if, ah, you might want to, ah—" Maybe he was half asleep from the way his mind and mouth couldn't communicate. "Are you busy Friday night?"

This time the lengthy pause was on her end. She finally said in a less sleepy voice, "Why?"

Why indeed? "I thought we could, ah, go out." He felt almost as awkward as the time he'd asked out Cindy Jo Hawkins on a date in eighth grade, his very first. She'd said yes.

"You mean, like a date?"

He thought about it. "Yeah, I guess that's what you'd call it."

"I thought you were seeing Edwina."

"That's on Saturday."

"No. I mean, I thought you two were seeing each other again. Hal said Edwina told him you guys were back together."

Mitch closed his eyes, wondering what else Eddie had told Hal. "No, we're not back together, nor will we ever be back together." He wondered if that was a sigh of relief he heard on Lydia's end of the line.

"Really? Why's that?"

"I didn't call to talk about Eddie and Hal. I called to ask you out on a date."

"Why?"

He scratched his head. That was a new one. No woman had ever asked him why before. They'd either accepted or they hadn't. Although on second thought, he realized with some surprise that he'd never been turned down.

"Well, because I'd like to spend some time with you."

"Why?"

"Did you grill Hal like this when *he* asked you out?"

"You're different than Hal."

"Thank God."

"Why, what's wrong with him?"

"Nothing. He's just a little—" *Cocky, arrogant, chauvinistic.*

"What?" she persisted.

"Let's just say he goes out with a lot of women."

"And you don't?"

She had him there. "Look, Lydia. I just want you to be careful with him. Don't let him pull anything with you that you're not comfortable with, okay?"

There was silence on the line. Then quietly, but with amusement in her voice, she asked, "Were you this protective of your kid brothers and sisters?"

"I'm not being protective," he said somewhat gruffly. "I'm just—" He was just what? He knew exactly what he was, and it was another new one for him. He was jealous.

"Look. Are you going out with me Friday or not?" he barked.

She had the nerve to laugh on her end of the line, which did nothing to improve his disposition. What she said improved it even less.

"No."

* * * *

"Mitch?" Lydia held out the phone in front of her face and looked at it, as if that would help. "Are you still there?"

"I'm still here. Don't mind me. I'm just sitting here licking my wounds."

"Oh, Mitch. I'd love to go out with you, but I need to stay home with Dad. It was hard enough trying to find someone to watch him Saturday night. Besides, I hate leaving him for two nights in a row."

"He's not a child, Lydia."

"I know. But still. I hate abandoning him."

"You're not abandoning him."

"That's what it feels like to me."

He didn't say anything.

She pulled a strand of hair in front of her face and peered at it, seeing a couple of split ends and trying to remember the last time she'd had it cut. She wasn't good about scheduling such things.

"You could come over here," she said. "We could barbecue something and rent a movie. I mean, Dad will be here, so it won't really be a date, but…"

"I grill a mean salmon," he said finally, and she pictured his crooked grin on the lips she had kissed only twice but yearned to kiss again.

"You told me that before."

"Are you saying I'm redundant?"

"That's a bad thing for a writer to be, I'm sure."

He chuckled, and she leaned back into the pillows, staring at the ceiling, remembering back to high school, when she'd longed to have lengthy telephone conversations with a boy with her bedroom door closed, just like all the other girls her age.

"So, you'll come over?"

"Okay, I'll come over," he said, "providing you answer a question that's been gnawing at me for the past fifteen minutes."

"What's that?"

"What are you wearing?"

* * * *

"You were right, Mitch. This salmon is to die for," Lydia said, taking another bite of the delicious fish.

He'd baked it on the grill with butter, lemon, beer, and top secret seasonings, he'd told her with a sly grin, wrapping the whole thing with foil. Her dad even seemed to enjoy it, and he wasn't usually a seafood fan.

"I'm glad you like it," Mitch said from across the table. "Although you never did answer my question."

She blushed all the way down to her toes, wondering why he was so interested in what she'd been wearing the other morning.

"What question?" her dad asked loudly from his place at the end of the table.

She popped another bite of salmon into her mouth to keep from having to answer, waving her hand at her father as if to tell him it was nothing interesting. The way Mitch watched her for the remainder of the meal suggested otherwise.

"So?" he asked as they washed the dishes after dinner, nudging her in the side. The delicious aroma of baking apples, cinnamon, and nutmeg pervaded the air from the apple crisp in the oven.

"So...what?" Even though she knew exactly so what.

"If you won't tell me, I'll have to guess."

"Why are you so interested?"

"Men need to know these things."

She loaded the plates in the dishwasher. "Oh, really? So I guess Hal will ask me the same thing on our date tomorrow night?"

His expression blackened. "He damn well better not."

"But it's okay for you to ask?"

He ignored her and scrubbed furiously at the pan even though it looked clean enough to her. "Forget I asked."

"The ugliest T-shirt you've ever seen."

He turned to her. "What?"

"That's what I sleep in. The ugliest T-shirt you've ever seen. Seriously, it's this horrid shade of green that goes totally hospital on me and—" At his quizzical look, she explained, "It makes me look like I should be hooked up to an IV or something."

"I doubt it's that bad."

"Oh, it is. Trust me."

He shook his head.

"Wanna bet?" she asked.

"What's the bet?"

"If it's not the ugliest thing you've ever seen, I'll buy you a triple-scoop ice-cream cone at Baskin-Robbins. But if it is, *you're* buying."

"I'll lie."

She giggled. "I'll be able to tell from your expression what you think."

He held out his wet, soapy hand, and they shook on it. Drying off with a dish towel, Lydia checked the timer on the stove. Fifteen minutes until the apple crisp was ready.

Lydia led the way upstairs. She paused in the doorway of her bedroom. "I suppose some men could take it wrong that I'm inviting you into my room."

His brows lifted. "Yeah, I wouldn't go inviting Hal up here tomorrow night. He's bound to get the wrong idea."

She nodded her head and grinned. "Your advice is duly noted, Teacher." She thought she saw him frown as he stepped past her into the bedroom.

"Cinderella's room," he muttered, walking to the windowed turret that overlooked the street.

"What?"

"When I first saw your house, it reminded me of a castle, and I wondered if you had the tower bedroom like Cinderella."

She crinkled up her nose. "You have a vivid imagination, don't you?"

He shrugged. "I'm a writer."

Shaking her head, she crossed to the bed and slipped her hand beneath the pillow. Grabbing the shirt, she hid it behind her back and said, "Ready?" She pulled it out with a flourish and held it by both shoulders so he could get the full effect.

The momentary flash of distaste in his eyes proved she'd won the bet.

"See? I told you," she said triumphantly.

He didn't even try to deny it. "I can't argue with you, Lydia," he said, staring at the shirt. "You know, all along I pegged you as someone with relatively good taste, but that—" He pointed at it. "'*N Sync?* Give me a break."

She giggled. "I liked them. It was the only concert I ever went to. I saved all my babysitting money to go and buy this shirt. Lance Bass was my favorite. I pretended he was singing directly to me." She fluttered her eyelashes.

"Isn't Lance Bass gay?"

"Well, yes, but nobody knew that back then. Guess I've always been attracted to secretly gay men." She got a dirty look for that.

"And why that color?"

"It accidentally went through the wash with Dad's new brown socks."

He didn't look completely convinced. "Okay, if you say so."

"I'd like a scoop of peanut butter and chocolate on the top and bottom, with a scoop of Daiquiri Ice sandwiched in between."

He grimaced. "Now I *know* you don't have good taste, Lydia. That combination sounds bad enough to choke a horse."

She smiled. "It's yummy. Trust me."

She shoved the ugly shirt back under the pillow and sat down on the bed. Mitch remained standing. She worried her lower lip, trying to figure out how to broach the next subject without looking totally naïve, even though she was just that.

"Remember how you told me that Hal dates a lot of women?"

"Yeah, why?"

"Were you trying to tell me that he, um, is kind of 'fast' with women?"

He sat down beside her, about a foot and a half separating them. The mattress sagged under his weight. "That would be one way to put it, yes."

"Well, um, how would I know?"

"How would you know what?"

She stared at her lap, clenching and unclenching her fists. "How will I know if he's putting the moves on me?"

"You'll know."

"No, really. I mean, if he actually *touches* me, I'll know, but otherwise what are the signs? What if he wants to kiss me, and I don't want him to? How will I know he wants to kiss me until he's right there in my face?" She peered over at him. "It's been forever since I've done this."

He reached his hand across the space separating them and rested it on her knee, squeezing softly. "First of all, remember a kiss is just a kiss."

Lydia's stomach lurched. She *knew* it. She'd been right about him, damn it.

"Second, relax. Hal may be experienced, but he's not going to do anything you don't want to do."

"How do you know?"

"Because if he does, he knows I'll kill him."

Surprised, she met his eyes. "You're serious, aren't you?"

"Damn right about that," he said, glancing away. He cleared his throat. "But back to your questions, I wouldn't worry too much. Your instincts will kick in."

"What if I was born without instincts?"

He didn't answer, so she turned her head and caught him looking at her mouth. Slowly, he leaned toward her. Her lips parted, and she leaned toward him, her gaze on his mouth, too.

His hand on her shoulder stopped her. "See? You knew."

She blinked. "Kn–Knew what?"

"That I wanted to kiss you."

Disappointment slammed into her. He didn't really want to kiss her. It was just another "lesson." She mentally composed herself and flung herself backward on the mattress, crossing her arms over her face.

"Maybe I should just cancel the stupid date. Hal asked me out expecting a date with a mature woman because I *look* like a mature woman. Little does he know he's dating Hannah Montana."

"Hannah Montana is cute." Mitch leaned onto his elbow, stretching out beside her. "You'll do fine," he said. "But how 'bout we stop talking about you and Hal?"

She moved her arm just enough to peer up at him. "Why? You jealous?" She was surprised at the coy tone in her voice.

"And how about you stop asking so many questions?"

"You planning on teaching me another lesson, Teacher?"

In one swift move, he removed her glasses and placed them next to her on the bed. Then he hovered over her until his breath mingled with hers. "You don't need any more lessons, Lydia. You just need to shut up and kiss me."

Chapter 10

Excitement danced along with Lydia's nerves as Mitch cupped her face with one of his large hands and tilted her head to better receive his kiss.

She didn't know if he was just doing this to help her out, but she no longer cared what his reason was. It only mattered that he was here with her now, and he was going to kiss her, something she'd been daydreaming and night-dreaming about since they'd kissed after the zucchini fight.

That time she'd been caught off guard by the electric feelings he brought about inside her. This time, she wasn't caught off guard but curious. She wanted this. She was ready for this.

She wrapped her fingers over his shoulders, pulling him close. His tongue swept along the seam of her mouth, and it felt natural to open up to him and take him inside. She moaned against his mouth. He tasted so good. This felt so right.

His hands slid to her shoulders and then around her back, pulling her tighter against him. Her breasts flattened against his hard chest, and his leg swept over hers as if claiming her.

A mild humming buzzed in her ears. Excitement roller-coastered through her veins, heating her skin and turning it hypersensitive. Even though she was completely out of practice, her body knew what to do. Her fingers raked gently over his shoulder blades, and his skin tightened as a shiver flowed through him. She smiled into the kiss, realizing he was turned on by her, which turned her on even more.

"You're driving me crazy, woman." The words vibrated against her mouth. He moved to kiss her jaw then down her neck. He tugged the collar of her T-shirt away to kiss and lick the sensitive area between her collarbones. "I want to do way more than just kiss you, Lydia."

Fire blazed through her veins at his words. "Like…what?" She couldn't believe how comfortable she felt with him.

He chuckled, and his hands skimmed over her breasts, through her shirt and bra, and her nipples immediately hardened at the contact. His thumbs leisurely traced their outlines. Her breathing shallowed.

"The list is long," he said. "And naughty."

She wriggled deeper into the mattress, and the move unexpectedly brought their hips together. The hard ridge of his erection pressed against the apex of her legs, and the area throbbed in response. "How naughty?"

He lifted up onto one elbow and peered down at her. "Lydia."

She saw his hesitation and the concern. "Stop treating me like I'm your fragile kid sister, Mitch. I might not have a ton of experience with this, but I'm a grown woman, and I know what I want."

He just stared at her. "Point taken," he finally muttered, his voice thick. He still made no further move to touch her.

She hooked her hand around his neck and pulled him down until his face was just an inch or so from hers. His warm breath fanned her lips. "How naughty?" she asked again.

He gazed into her eyes a long moment, then his eyes narrowed, a grin tugged at one corner of his mouth, and he kissed her long and deep. His hand slid under her shirt at the waist, then worked the front clasp of her bra. Pushing the flimsy garment aside, he cupped his hand over her bare breast. She arched her back, pressing into his hot palm. He broke the kiss and lowered his head to kiss between her breasts. When his hot mouth closed over her nipple, she gasped and shoved her fingers into his hair, holding him there.

Soft moans slipped from her lips at the exquisite sensation. Pleasure points shot through all her nerve endings and gathered between her legs in a steady, persistent throbbing. Her heels pressed into the mattress as he nibbled and suckled on her, pulling her nipple deeper into his mouth. She dragged his head closer, wanting— needing—more.

As if understanding that need, his hand slid down her belly and found the waistband of her jeans. He tugged at the button then paused and lifted his head from her breast.

He groaned and rolled off of her. The air-conditioning blasted her bare torso like a snowstorm in the middle of summer. Her damp nipples felt raw and exposed.

"Did I do something wrong?" she whispered, tugging down her shirt. Embarrassment crept upward from her feet.

Mitch's expression was both gentle and exasperated. "You did nothing wrong, my sweet." He reached for her hand and entwined their fingers. He turned his head and stared up at the slow-moving ceiling fan. "You did everything just right."

She couldn't stop the smile from pulling wide on her mouth. "Really?"

"Oh yeah." He squeezed her hand. "But the timer on the oven is going off right now."

She lifted her head and listened. So it was. She rested her head back on the pillow and watched the faux-wood blades of the fan go around and around until her pulse slowed to an almost normal rate.

Finally, she said, "I'm not in the mood for apple crisp anymore. But I am in the mood for something."

He turned his face toward her, his eyes questioning and faintly suggestive. "Oh, yeah? What?"

She sat up, the mattress squeaking with the movement. "Ice cream."

* * * *

"A bet's a bet," Lydia told Mitch as he helped load Robert into the backseat of their old Explorer.

Ice cream wasn't exactly at the top of the list of things he wanted in his mouth right now, but she was right. A bet was a bet. Besides, he didn't know that he was ready to take their relationship to the next level. When that buzzer had gone off, a part of him had been relieved.

This was unchartered territory for him. He'd never stopped himself from pursuing a sexual relationship with a woman before. If it led to that, and both parties were willing, then great. It was different with Lydia though. *She* was different. If they made love, there would be no turning back for her, and if he was honest with himself, there would be no turning back for him.

He didn't have time to ponder the implications of that revelation, because Lydia had asked him a question. She held out the keys, her brows lifted, so he figured she must've asked him to drive.

He snatched the dangling keys from her, circled the vehicle, and climbed into the driver's seat. The seat cushions were worn and not too comfortable. This vehicle had obviously given the St. Clairs their money's worth. A quick glance at the odometer read 180,000 miles. Wow. He didn't think he'd ever kept a car beyond 50,000 miles, and even that was pushing it.

During the drive, Lydia's hands stayed folded primly in her lap, like a schoolgirl, but that's certainly not how he thought of her. His gaze grazed her lips, which were parted slightly. With a quick lift of his eyebrows, he returned his eyes to the road.

The feel of her mouth against his and the feel and taste of her nipples were imprinted on his mind, would stay that way for some time, he was sure.

At the ice cream store, he unfolded Robert's wheelchair from the back of the van and looked on as Lydia helped her dad into it. She was obviously well practiced in this maneuver, as she was quick and efficient.

He thought of the calls he had made for Robert, the ones to local retirement homes, and guilt welled inside of him. Lydia wasn't like him. She obviously didn't feel the burden of caring for her father as he had as a young man in charge of all his younger siblings. He'd been resentful as hell. She seemed content and at peace.

She was quite a woman.

As promised, Lydia ordered three scoops with pale green Daiquiri Ice between the peanut butter and chocolate. The young clerk didn't bat an eye at the odd combination as he handed it across the counter.

Her eyes bright, Lydia licked the bottom scoop, her tongue licking around the cone. She closed her eyes. "Mmm. Pure heaven."

He imagined her tongue licking around parts of him. Mitch almost groaned.

Robert ordered one scoop of French vanilla in a bowl, and Mitch requested a double scoop of Pralines and Cream.

"That's boring," Lydia said, watching the clerk scoop up his order.

"It's what I get every time."

"You need to be more daring, Mitch. Branch out. Try new things."

He could tell she was having him on. "What is this, pupil teaching the teacher?"

A veiled look shadowed her eyes a moment then was gone so fast he wasn't sure he'd actually seen it.

"You're telling me you don't always get that combination when you come here?" He motioned to her tilting cone.

She lapped at the ice cream, chocolate coating her lips. "'Always' doesn't apply. This is the first time I've been here in years."

That thought saddened him. He'd bring her here weekly if it brought that sublime expression of pleasure to her face. He wanted to introduce her to many new things, many new pleasures, and not all of them involved ice cream. Okay, so none of them involved ice cream.

The threesome nabbed a free table in the corner, Robert's wheelchair pushed up as close as possible and facing the window.

Robert struggled to put spoon to bowl to mouth, Mitch noticed, but also saw that Lydia seemed blind to it. Each bite was a painstaking ordeal, almost painful to watch. He had to refrain from reaching over and spoon-feeding the man. How humiliating for this formerly independent man, a man who still possessed sound mind and faculty, to be reduced to eating as messily as a small child. How even more humiliating were he, Mitch, to step in and help.

At one point, Robert's spoon didn't quite hit the ice cream but instead grazed the side of the small cardboard bowl, causing it to slip sideways across the table and fall onto the floor, the ice cream splattering across the tiles, the wheels of the chair and Mitch's pant leg.

Robert muttered a string of obscenities, Mitch leapt back in surprise, and Lydia calmly rose to fetch a stack of napkins.

Mitch didn't know what to say to the old man, whose eyes stared blindly out the window as if unaware of what had happened. White cream was smeared on his lips like a toddler, but Mitch was surprised at the hint of moisture rimming the man's eyes as Lydia proceeded to wipe his mouth and then the mess on the floor. Mitch grabbed a few napkins and cleaned up the splatters on the wheelchair and table.

"Oh, Mitch." She pointed out the stains on his pant legs. "I'm sorry," she said, her voice just above a whisper. She dabbed at them with the wad of napkins.

He stopped her with a gentle hand on her wrist. "I can do that."

After a moment, she straightened and returned to her chair.

When he'd finished his small bit of cleaning up, he turned to Lydia's dad. "Can I get you another bowl?"

Robert shook his head ever so slightly, the movement jerky.

"I never really liked the French vanilla here anyway," Mitch joked and patted Robert's knee, feeling bad for him and for Lydia.

Speaking of, she watched him with a strange expression on her face. A sweet smile danced along her lips. After a moment, she returned her focus to her ice cream, eating it quietly until it was gone.

"Do you realize you finished three giant scoops, and I haven't even finished my measly two?" he asked her.

"My daughter's always had…a hollow leg when it comes to ice cream," Robert chimed in with a gruff voice. "She'd probably eat yours, too, if you'd let her."

Lydia's eyes twinkled at the return of her father's good humor. "I've never tried Pralines and Cream."

"Seriously?" Mitch asked. "Well, here. You can't have the rest, so don't even *think* about it, but you may have a taste." He stretched his arm across the table. She wrapped her fingers around his hand and licked around the remaining scoop.

* * * *

Right up until the time Hal King rang her doorbell, Lydia debated canceling on him. For one, she was as nervous as that mouse she and Mitch had trapped—this was the first real date she'd been on in years. Second, while Hal might be a King, she wasn't sure he was anywhere near the vicinity of Prince Charming. The third and most important reason she had for not wanting to go out on a date with Hal was that she was in love with another man.

She'd realized it last night after the ice cream parlor, and, of course, after the tryst on her bed. Wow. She'd never felt so alive in her life. Mitch made her feel like she'd never hoped to feel, the way she'd read about in romance books and seen in the movies. For those moments as he'd kissed her and caressed her body, he'd made her believe that fairy tales might actually exist. He'd given her the hope that maybe, just maybe, dreams do come true.

It was later at the ice cream parlor when the depth of her feelings had slapped her upside the head. He'd been so kind and non-patronizing with her dad. He hadn't acted at all embarrassed or put out with her father's difficulties. He'd fit right in, acting like part of the family. She'd realized she loved him for that.

After last night, she'd hoped Mitch would ask her to cancel her date with Hal. She'd hoped he'd tell her that he cared for her and didn't want her to date another man.

She tried really hard not to get carried away with her emotions and her newly realized love for him. He'd told her himself last night that a kiss was just a kiss, that most men didn't make much of it other than a pleasant pastime.

While she tried to do the same, she was failing miserably. It meant *everything* to her. Still, she was the first to admit she wasn't exactly an expert at dating and men. She might be madly in love with him, but he might not feel anything more than friendship toward her.

Still, she'd hoped he'd call today. He hadn't.

When the door bell rang at promptly 7:30 p.m., she was ready with purse in hand and dressed in what she hoped was proper first-date attire.

* * * *

The wind hissed against Mitch's face as his Harley cruised up the mountain roads outside of Boise. The evening bugs swarmed, and he kept getting zinged in the cheek, chin, and forehead by the little critters.

He paid them no mind, just pushed his bike harder, his hand gripped tight on the throttle. He hadn't been able to relax and enjoy the baseball game with Eddie tonight, because all he could think about was Lydia. While the Hawks ran up the score, Hal King might be trying to score with her.

He wondered where Hal had taken her on their date. Probably some fancy-schmancy restaurant to impress her, something Mitch had never thought of doing. Hell, the only place he'd ever taken her was Baskin-Robbins. Real classy.

Damn. She was being wined and dined by one of Boise's biggest Casanovas, and Mitch had never gotten around to doing that. He wanted to wine and dine her. He wanted to treat her like a princess. She deserved that.

Their kiss last night had clarified something he'd been denying for a while. He'd fallen for her and fallen for her hard.

It scared the crap out of him. He didn't have time for a serious relationship. He liked his life just the way it was. He'd been telling himself that for years.

He'd also shared an ice-cream cone with her last night, something he swore he'd never do.

He'd been telling himself *that* for years, too.

* * * *

Back at his house, Mitch popped open a beer and headed to the patio. He sat on a chaise lounge and stared out at the night. Lights from Boise's skyline twinkled in the distance. The eerie howl of a coyote echoed off the foothills.

He glanced at his watch, barely readable in the night shadows. Eleven p.m. The date should be over. It damn well better be over. Lydia wouldn't want to be out too late, to leave her dad for too long. Her loyalty to her dad was reassuring and a welcome thing.

He chugged the beer. Maybe he'd get drunk, something he rarely did, and something he never did alone. Tonight, though, drunk sounded damn good, especially when he pictured Hal walking Lydia to her house, taking her into his arms on the veranda, pressing his mouth to hers.

He crushed the empty can in his fist. It should be *him* kissing her, not Hal. Not some guy who could never offer her anything beyond a good time.

What could *he* offer her beyond that? Was he really any better than Hal?

* * * *

He called her the next morning almost early enough to be

considered rude.

"So?" he barked.

"So…what?" Her smile drifted across the line.

"So, smarty-pants, how was the hot date?" That was difficult for him to even say.

"We had a nice time. Hal was the perfect gentleman."

That's a first. Mitch frowned. "Did he…make any moves on you?" It was really none of his business, but he had to know if Hal kissed her. For some reason, he really had to know that.

He held his breath waiting for the answer.

"A lady never kisses and tells. You should know that by now," she chided him gently.

If he'd been there, he would've shaken her for that prim answer. "Did you kiss him, Lydia?"

"Like I said, he was the perfect—"

"Yeah, yeah," he snarled. "You said that already. He was just a prince. I got it. You seeing him again?"

"Why? Are you jealous?"

"No!" By the long pause that followed, he figured he'd said that too quickly.

In a more muted voice she said, "Hal offered to be my date to the reunion."

This time the long pause was on his end of the line. Long fingers of jealousy reached inside his chest and wrenched his heart. "What? Did you ask him?"

"No. He was so sweet. I told him my reunion was next weekend and how I probably wouldn't go because I hadn't lined up a date, and he offered to go with me. Wasn't that nice of him?"

Peachy. "Gee. What a swell guy."

"Is something wrong?"

"No. Why would anything be wrong?"

"Because you're acting really weird."

"I'm just surprised, that's all."

"Why? The reason I originally met you was because I wanted a date to my reunion. You even gave me 'lessons' to meet a man. Now that I have a date, I would think you'd be happy for me. Unless you have a reason not to be happy about it…"

He felt about an inch tall, and he sighed. "You're right. I'm sorry. I'm being a jerk. I guess I can't help thinking it should be me taking you to the reunion."

"You? Why?"

"I don't know. Because…because…" *Come on, Gannon, you're a writer, for Christ's sake. You should be able to give her a reasonable answer to her question.* What he came up with was, "Just because."

"Well, I would love for you to take me, but you can't change your plans, remember?"

"I remember." If this wasn't the tenth year in a row he and his buddies did the Harley road trip, and if any of the guys had ever canceled on it before, and if he didn't look forward to this trip all year long…

He cleared his throat. "Well, I'm glad you found someone, Lydia."

"Thank you," she said, sounding miffed.

He couldn't blame her. He was acting like a spurned teenager.

"But I still have one question," he said.

"What?"

"Did he kiss you?" *And, more importantly, did you kiss him back?*

* * * *

Monday evening after work, Lydia had just said good-bye to the day's caregiver when the phone rang.

"May I speak to Mitch Gannon, please?" asked the female voice.

Lydia's brows drew together. "Uh, he doesn't live here."

"Oh. Hmm. This is the number I have."

"Well, I know Mitch. He's a, ah, friend of the family. I can give you his number."

"Who am I speaking with?" the woman asked.

"Lydia St. Clair."

"Are you related to a Mr. Robert St. Clair?"

"He's my dad."

"Well, then, I can certainly give this message to you. My name is Marian Barstow. I'm the director of resident relations at the Morning Glory Retirement Villa. Mr. Gannon was in here recently inquiring about an apartment for your father. At the time we didn't have…"

Heat flamed her face, and her pulse pounded a sharp staccato in her ears. Lydia didn't hear the rest of the woman's words. Mitch had inquired about rooms for her dad. He wanted him out of the picture. How stupid had she been?

"Ms. St. Clair?"

Lydia had forgotten she was still on the phone. "I'm sorry. What did you say?"

"I asked if you'd seen our facility before. It's really quite beautiful, and I'd be happy to—"

"No. That won't be necessary."

"Yes, our reputation does speak for itself."

"I'm sure it does, but I'm not interested in placing my father in a facility. He will be staying with me."

"I'm confused. When Mr. Gannon visited, he told me that—"

"Mr. Gannon was mistaken. Thank you for calling."

She slammed down the phone and sat at the kitchen table, glad her father was in the other room and couldn't see what must be complete shock and betrayal on her face. Her stomach churned like the wash machine whirring in the next room. Bile burned her throat.

As if the events from the past few weeks were on a movie screen inside her head, her mind replayed some key scenes. When Mitch asked her if she'd consider a nursing home for her dad. When he'd told her he liked his life simple and not full of responsibility. Edwina's revelation that he didn't date single moms. His disappointment when he wanted to take her for a spontaneous ride on his Harley and she couldn't go because of her dad.

Robert St. Clair cramped Mitch's style, obviously. If he was to have a relationship with her, he didn't want her dad around.

She didn't know whether to cry or throw something.

She'd thought he was different. All his considerate actions toward her father had just been an act. He'd been buying time. All the while he'd slowly oozed his way into her heart, he'd been trying to find a place to dump her father, to get him out of the way.

She felt more betrayed right now than she had when she'd learned he was straight. That had been more about humiliation mixed with a little bit of jubilation that she was allowed to feel attracted to him. This…well, this was much worse. Her chest felt empty inside, a big, gaping hole where her stupid, trusting heart used to be.

* * * *

Mitch stood at Lydia's front door, his hand poised to knock. Something hadn't been right in her tone when she'd called him and asked him to stop by after work, even though she knew he worked until midnight.

Seeing lights through the paned door, he knocked. After a few moments, footsteps resounded from inside the house. Then the door swung open.

Lydia glared at him from the other side of the screen, not even the faintest hint of welcome on her face. His bad feeling elevated to red-alert status even before she didn't invite him inside.

"Is everything all right?" That was a stupid question when clearly something was wrong. Very wrong.

She pressed a palm to the screen door, as if using it for a barrier. "I got an interesting call this evening," she said.

"Oh?"

She nodded, her blue eyes not quite meeting his gaze. "Do you know a Marian Barstow?"

Although the name sounded faintly familiar, he couldn't place it. He shook his head slowly, wondering where this was going and not liking it. "The name rings a bell. Who is she?"

"She works at Morning Glory, the new retirement home out near Kuna."

He froze. From her icy gaze, he could tell she wouldn't understand anything he told her. "Lydia, let me explain."

"What? You want to tell me how you went behind my back to find a 'suitable' home for my father? You want to give me a good reason why you went against my wishes after I have repeatedly told you how important it is for my dad to stay with me? You want to explain how, with my dad out of the way, we'll have time to actually date?"

"It's not like that at all," he began, at a loss both in words and spirit.

She crossed her arms over her chest and widened her stance, as if preparing for battle. "Okay. Tell me what it's like."

He motioned to the swing at the end of the porch. "Do you want to—"

"No. Go on."

How could he tell her that her father was so worried about her that he'd asked Mitch to look into assisted-living facilities? How could he tell her he could see it wasn't just the fear of abandoning her dad, but her fear of being alone? How could he tell her *anything* when she glowered at him with blatant hatred in her eyes?

"The truth shouldn't take so long to explain," she said.

"It's not that simple."

"You've lied to me from day one, Mitch. Just this once tell me the truth. Tell me why you did this."

"It's not because I want to get your dad out of the way. I like him."

Her expression said she didn't believe him.

He wanted to tell her the truth, that Robert had asked this favor of him, but then he'd be betraying him, too. He'd given the man his word. "I think you should talk to your dad."

She shook her head. "I won't tell him about this. He'll be too disappointed in you. He likes you, you know? How could you do this to him?"

"You mean how could I do this to you, don't you?" he asked softly.

Moisture glistened in her eyes, and she looked away. "I guess I should have known better, but I trusted you. I believed you. I even started to think that I I—"

His heart skipped a beat. "That you what?"

She swiped at her cheek with the back of one hand. "In some warped way, I have to blame myself. All the signs were there. You told me yourself that you didn't like responsibility and that my caring for my dad would be a big deterrent to meeting men. You told me that from the start. Edwina warned me that you didn't date single women because of the responsibility and that you'd broken up with her because of her son."

"That's not true."

She went on as if he hadn't spoken. "You told me how relieved you were to be rid of your younger brothers and sisters, how resentful you were, that they'd been a burden. I heard all that but didn't listen. I wanted to believe the best." She met his eyes. "I wanted to believe in the fairy tale, that Prince Charming really does exist. But he doesn't, does he?"

Mitch felt as if his heart had been ripped out of his chest and slammed against a brick wall. How could he respond to that? Especially when she had most of it right.

A tear slipped down her cheek, and she didn't bother wiping it away. "See? You can't come up with an appropriate response, can you?" She reached for the door behind her. "Good-bye."

He opened the screen door and pushed against the solid one before she could shut it. "First of all, I think your dad is great and would never do anything to hurt him or you. Second, I broke up with Eddie not because she has a child but because she's self-absorbed and selfish and because I couldn't see myself enjoying anything beyond the short-term with her."

"Are you finished?" Her stare was dull and lifeless.

"No, I'm not." He glanced upward for courage then met her gaze square. "This mission of yours to go back to your reunion as a changed person is ridiculous." She tried to shut the door on him, but he wouldn't let her. "You're so caught up in pretending to be something you're not, you don't realize everything you have. Sure, your life might not be totally under your control right now, but you have something lots of people don't—someone to come home to each night, a father who loves you so much he's willing to—" He cleared his throat. "Your life is worthy of respect just the way it is," he added softly.

"And the reason you went behind my back to call that retirement home?"

He closed his eyes and sighed. "I can't tell you that."

A tear spilled from the inner corner of her eye. "I thought not. Good-bye, Mitch."

This time when she tried to shut the door in his face, he let her.

Chapter 11

Early Friday evening, Mitch returned home from work hoping to find a message from Lydia on his machine. He'd called her several times over the past couple of days, but she wouldn't take his calls or return them. He could just show up at her house unannounced, but from her anger the other night, he knew she needed some time.

He turned on his computer and sorted through his e-mail. At the bottom of the first screen, the subject line displayed the title of his book, which meant just one thing. Shit. Another rejection.

He clicked on the message and saw he was right. This time, however, the editor had been kind enough to write a personal response rather than a form rejection letter.

It said his plot was intriguing, his writing style fresh, but his characters were flat. Mitch hit the delete button. Rejections no longer stung as much as they used to. Rather, they gave him new resolve. Not wanting the e-mail to get the best of him, he opened his word processor.

He pounded out his next scene, fingers flying across the keyboard. After about twenty minutes, he stopped. The problem with his story hit him like a wayward baseball pitch. His main character *was* flat. The guy didn't care about anything except himself and the crime at hand. He didn't "feel."

With a gush of inspiration that some writers only dream about, Mitch's right brain took over, and he started rewriting the book from page one. First, he added a girlfriend. Initially, she was there just to add complexity and depth to the main character's life. Then, out of the blue, his main character was in love, and from there the story just flew.

The sky had darkened outside, and Mitch was fifty pages into the story inside his head when he had another realization.

His life was flat, too.

Pushing away from the computer, he glanced around at his house at the expensive furnishings, at his high-powered entertainment system, his office setup, his things.

That's all they were—things. This was just a house. It wasn't a home, not even close. All these years he'd told himself his life was just how he liked it—he could spend his money how he wanted, do what he wanted to do when he wanted to do it. He was happy with his lifestyle.

He had been until he met Lydia.

None of his things—not even his writing—seemed important anymore. They were so trivial, so meaningless, just as his life would be again without her.

Another realization snuck up on him, then hit him hard. He was in love with Lydia St. Clair.

He had to talk to her.

Moments later, the beep of her answering machine rang in his ear. "Hi, Lydia. If you're there, please pick up." He waited. "I…just wanted to tell you to have a good time at your reunion tomorrow night, and I hope it's everything you dreamed it would be." If Hal laid a hand on her, he'd kill him with his bare hands.

"I don't leave on my road trip until noon, so if you want to call me before then…" He cleared his throat, feeling like an idiot, pretty sure she was home listening to his message as he spoke it. "Anyway, I hope you'll call me. I really need to talk to you."

Mitch hung up the phone, never feeling so empty and lonely in his life.

* * * *

The machine clicked off, and Mitch's message ended. Lydia stared at the phone, her arms wrapped around herself. She'd replayed that message several times since he'd called her last night. Each time she heard his voice, her resolve crumbled a bit more. This time, she even started to reach for the phone, wanting to hear his voice, wanting to hear an explanation for what he did. She dropped her hand. There was no explanation.

"Call him."

She turned to find her dad watching her from his wheelchair. "I don't want to talk to him, Dad."

"Yes…you do," he rasped. "You're in love with him, aren't you?"

Her eyes widened. "That obvious, eh?"

"To my old eyes it is. Call him. He's obviously anxious…to talk to you."

"I can't. I don't know that I could ever talk to him again."

"Why? What did he do that's so bad that you won't answer his calls?"

She shook her head. "I can't tell you."

"Is it a private sexual thing?"

She couldn't help smirking at that. "No."

"Does he have an incurable disease?"

"No, Dad."

"Then you can tell me."

She sighed, hesitant to tell him, but needing to talk to someone about this. "Remember how I told you he won't date women with children?"

"You also told me you didn't believe that."

"I didn't, but…" She stared out the window to the garden Mitch had helped her tame. "He wanted me to put you in a nursing home, Dad. He went behind my back and did some research on them. I know this isn't very nice, but apparently he wasn't comfortable dating me with you around."

Her dad looked away and stared out the kitchen window, not

saying anything.

"I know that must hurt. It surprised me, too." Her voice caught. "But you don't have to worry. I would never do that to you. Ever."

"I put him up to it."

She blinked. "What?"

Her father met her gaze with clear eyes. "I asked Mitch to look into some local nursing and retirement homes for me."

Lydia pressed a hand to her heart, feeling faint. "You did? Why?"

"Because you...wouldn't do it for me. Because I feel like a burden to you. Because I see you wasting your life taking care of me."

Tears streamed down her face, and she rushed to him, knelt, and rested her head in his lap. "Oh, Dad. I love you. I've never thought of you as a burden."

He stroked her hair like he used to when she was a little girl. "I'm sorry, sss...sweetheart. I shouldn't have done what I did, and I tell you, Mitch was not happy about it."

She looked up. "He wasn't?"

Robert shook his gray head and cleared his throat. "I kind of, ah, forced him to do it. I, ah, told him I didn't have long to live...had a bad heart, that it would make me happy to see my girl happy." He gave her a sheepish half smile. "That sort of thing."

Lydia closed her eyes, thinking of all she'd accused Mitch of and wondering, hoping, if he might possibly care for her after all.

"Call him."

She glanced at the clock, and her heart sank. 1:00 p.m. "He's already left."

"He has a cell phone, doesn't he?"

She dialed his number. As it rang, her dad said, "Can you forgive this old man for...messing everything up?"

She figured she should be angry with her father, but right now all she could think about was reaching Mitch and setting things right with him. She smiled at her dad, and Mitch's voicemail picked up.

"Mitch? Hi. It's Lydia. When you get this, please call me. Please. I want to talk to you, too."

She hung up the phone and turned to her dad. "Well. I guess I'll have to wait until he gets home." She glanced again at the clock. "In the meantime, I need to start getting ready for my big night." Funny how she wasn't as excited as she thought she'd be.

She hadn't reached the foyer when the phone rang. She practically sprinted back into the kitchen. "Hello?"

"Say, Lydia. It's Hal. I'm afraid I've got some bad news."

* * * *

The entourage of rumbling Harleys pulled into Cactus Pete's casino in Jackpot, Nevada. Mitch and his friends always made their first stop here to stretch their legs and do a bit of gambling.

"You guys go ahead," Mitch said as the group approached the entrance. He pulled his cell phone from the zippered pocket of his leather jacket. "I need to check in at work. Save a seat at the blackjack table for me." He speed dialed the bar without needing to look at the screen.

"The Alley," came Eddie's bored voice over the line.

"Hey, Eddie. Is Ben around?" Ben was his assistant manager.

"He's on his lunch break. I thought you were gone."

"I am. I'm in Jackpot. I forgot to tell him that we're almost out of paper towels for the bathrooms. We're also running low on decaf. He'll need to do a Costco run."

"Okay, I'll tell him. Oh, guess what? You know that story Hal's been working on, the one about the senator?"

"Vaguely, why?"

"Well, the story just broke. He's flying to DC this afternoon. He was pretty jazzed about it."

"What? Hal's leaving town? But he's supposed to take Lydia to her reunion."

He heard the pop of Edwina's bubble gum. "Guess the poor thing won't be going after all, unless she wants to show up alone." She chuckled, as if amused by Lydia's situation.

Anger toward Eddie's callous attitude and sadness over Lydia's predicament warred in his chest. He hung up the phone, staring at the tiny screen as the call disconnected. Poor Lydia had been dreaming about this night for weeks.

* * * *

Lydia had been dreaming about this night for weeks. She'd dreamed of arriving in a carriage, or at least a fancy car, with a handsome prince helping her out with a courtly bow and debonair manner. Instead, she'd driven herself in her eleven-year-old Ford Explorer.

At least she had a great dress. She gathered up the skirt of her gown in both hands and wriggled out of the SUV. She slammed the door shut and adjusted the bodice of the gown. She wasn't used to having half her boobs on display. At least the weather was warm.

Adjusting the thin strap of her silver purse over her shoulder, she stepped away from the vehicle. Or at least she tried to. Her skirt had caught in the door.

Opening the door enough to pull free, she noticed the greasy stain marring the shimmery fabric. She closed her eyes momentarily and had a very short pity party that she was facing her ten-year reunion without a date and with a grease stain on her once-perfect dress.

She glanced at the hotel across the street where all her classmates were milling about inside somewhere. She didn't have to go. She could just go home and change back into her jeans and T-shirt, move back into her comfort zone and have no life again.

Straightening her shoulders, she pressed her lips together. If she didn't do this, she'd spend the rest of her life, or at least the time it took to down a Costco-sized bag of Cheetos by herself, wishing she hadn't been such a wuss.

She remembered Mitch's words about her life being okay just the way it was. She had a lot to be proud of. If her classmates didn't agree, so what?

She took a deep breath. Okay. She could to do this. Grease stain be damned.

Her bravado was short-lived. She entered the hotel and headed for the ballroom on the top floor. In the elevator, everyone stared at her. Was it the grease stain? Glancing down at her full skirt, it seemed pretty well hidden in the folds.

The elevator doors opened to a registration area where tables were set up with nametags. A big sign in front of her read, *Welcome Class of '01.* The room was crowded with people talking, laughing, and apparently having a good time. As she stepped out of the elevator, everyone turned to stare at her. Actually, "gawk" would be the more appropriate term. She immediately knew why. She was the only one wearing formal attire. Everyone else was dressed in jeans and cowboy boots.

Oh God.

This was worse than showing up at her senior prom alone and without a date. Those condescending looks were nothing compared to this. Lydia's face heated up, and she turned around to dive back into the elevator, but the doors had closed, and from the looks of the lighted floor numbers, the elevator was on its way down.

Closing her eyes for courage and wisdom, she took a deep breath before turning back around to face her former classmates. Pasting a smile on her face and hoping she didn't look as completely ridiculous as she felt, she headed toward the registration table.

The woman behind the table looked up as Lydia approached, running her gaze up and down the silver gown. Lydia waited for the snide remark.

The woman said, "Great dress."

Lydia blinked at the seemingly sincere compliment. "Um, thank you. I, ah, forgot my cowboy boots."

The woman laughed. "You obviously didn't get the letter from the reunion committee saying we decided to go with our country roots and go Western rather than formal? It was posted on our Facebook page, too."

Lydia remembered the envelopes she'd tossed, assuming she wasn't going to attend, and her stomach churned. "I, uh, don't do Facebook."

"Yeah, I shouldn't either. Huge time-suck."

Lydia noticed the woman's nametag. Cissy McAllister. She'd been cheerleader, homecoming queen, and one of Lydia's biggest nemeses. She was still very pretty, although she'd put on a few pounds.

"Don't feel too bad. You're not the only one who didn't get the notice. There's a guy here who showed up in a tux. Maybe you two can hook up and look elegant together." Cissy smiled. "I don't recognize you. What's your name?" Her hands hovered over the nametags, ready to grab the appropriate one.

Lydia took a deep breath. "Lydia St. Clair."

Cissy's brows furrowed as if trying to remember. "Gosh, I guess my memory isn't so good these days. Did we know each other?"

"Oh, you knew me. I was the girl whose clothes you used to steal out of my P.E. locker and hang in the shower."

Cissy's hand flew to her mouth. "That was you? Oh, my God. You've changed. I would never have recognized you. I'm so sorry about how we treated you. My friends and I really were bitches, weren't we? Thank God I grew up."

Lydia stared at Cissy then couldn't help smiling. "It was a long time ago."

Cissy looked relieved. She turned to a woman at the next table. "Bonnie. Come over here a sec." Turning back to Lydia, she said, "Do you remember Bonnie Mason?"

Of course Lydia remembered her. Bonnie was one of Cissy's

cronies, another of the popular crowd who had wanted nothing to do with the likes of her. She braced herself for a nasty look or comment.

"Bonnie, this is Lydia St. Clair. Do you remember her?"

Bonnie stared at Lydia, and her eyes widened. "Oh, my God. I was so mean to you. I'm so embarrassed. Awesome dress, by the way. I had a fabulous one of my own picked out. Then the reunion committee went and changed the dress code, damn them." She laughed.

And so it went. Lydia moved through the crowd, feeling conspicuous in her silver gown, but more comfortable than she'd ever thought possible. The worst moment came when Roger Gilmore, a particularly nasty memory from her past, stepped in front of her.

Lydia squared her shoulders and lifted her chin, pleased her high heels put her at eye level with her former tormentor.

His wobbly grin told her he was half drunk already. "Well, if it isn't Lydia-Chlamydia. My, how you've grown up."

Ten years ago, that name had made her cry. Now she thought about how Mitch might answer such a comment. "My, how you haven't." She spun away, her gown rustling against her legs.

A little while later, as she mingled with a group of classmates she'd been in yearbook with, a flash of black and white caught her eye. She recalled Cissy's words that someone else had arrived completely overdressed, and she turned to see who might be feeling as out of place as she.

Mitch's dark eyes sparkled in the chandelier lights overhead. His perfectly cut tuxedo accentuated his incredible physique. Her stomach somersaulted.

"Mitch?" she asked as he approached, not really believing it was him.

He stepped in front of her, holding her gaze. "Hey, gorgeous." His eyes swept over her. "And boy, do you look gorgeous."

She blushed. "I thought you were gone."

"I was. I got as far as Jackpot and had to call the bar for

something. Eddie told me Hal canceled on you."

"And you came all the way back to meet me here?" Tears pooled in her lower eyelids, blurring her vision.

"I came back to save you, but I see you've already saved yourself." He nodded his head toward the rest of the group.

She blinked back a threatening tear. "But your road trip means a lot to you."

"It does. But not nearly as much as you do." He peered deep into her eyes, and her heart flip-flopped in her chest.

"Really?" Her voice sounded breathy, even to her own ears.

"Really." He leaned forward and whispered in her ear, "Dance with me."

He tucked her hand into his and led her onto the parquet dance floor where the band onstage played a slow country ballad about true love.

Mitch wrapped his arm around her waist, and she laid a hand atop his shoulder. He brought their other hands together between them, heart to heart. She reveled in the feel of his warm, hard body against hers.

"I stopped by your house a bit ago," he said, "and imagine my surprise when your dad told me you'd come here alone. I'm proud of you."

"I could never have done so without your encouragement."

He used their joined hands to tip up her chin. "You're an amazing woman, Lydia St. Clair." He kissed her softly upon the mouth. "Your dad told me you two had a talk."

"I'm sorry I doubted you, Mitch. Forgive me?"

"I will on one condition."

"What's that?"

He grinned and spun her across the floor, slowing when they reached a darkened and relatively private corner. "Marry me."

This time she couldn't stop the tears from falling onto her cheeks. "What?"

He chuckled and nuzzled the tender area behind her ear, causing the most exquisite shiver to race across her body. "I'm head over heels in love with you, Lydia St. Clair. I want to make a home with you. I want go to bed with you each night and wake up to you each morning. I want to make love to you until your head spins."

As if to prove that last point, he brushed his thumbs across the exposed swells of her breasts, causing her nipples to strain against the confines of her strapless bra.

"I want to make love to you until *my* head spins," he said, his voice husky. "I want to have babies with you, my sweet. I'm talking happily ever after. You, me, and your dad, if you'll both have me. What do you say? Could I be your lifetime prince?"

She brushed a tear from her cheek with the back of her hand and reached up to cup his face in her palms. His eyes glistened in the shadows.

"I'd like nothing more in this world," she whispered against his mouth and gave him a kiss that surpassed the most romantic fairy tale.

THE END

WWW.REBECCAJCLARK.COM

ABOUT THE AUTHOR

Rebecca J. Clark is a sucker for a happy ending. She loves the feeling she gets after reading a great romance novel—just for that moment, everything is right in the world. When she's not writing, she works as a personal fitness trainer and group-exercise instructor. All the exercise supports her voracious Cheetos® and chocolate habits. She makes her home in the Pacific Northwest with her husband of 24 years, two kids, a German-shepherd beast who thinks he's a lap dog, two rats, two cats who plot to kill the beast and eat the rats, and a gecko. In her free time, Rebecca enjoys reading, watching *Criminal Minds* reruns on TV, and doing absolutely nothing.

BookStrand

www.BookStrand.com

CPSIA information can be obtained at www.ICGtesting.com
Printed in the USA
BVOW08s0052110515

399705BV00008B/173/P